Ruthless Hearts 2

Willie Slaughter

Lock Down Publications and Ca$h Presents

Ruthless Hearts 2

A Novel by *Willie Slaughter*

Lock Down Publications
P.O. Box 870494
Mesquite, Tx 75187

Visit our website @
www.lockdownpublications.com

First Edition March 2020
Printed in the United States of America

Lock Down Publications
Like our page on Facebook: Lock Down Publications @
www.facebook.com/lockdownpublications.ldp
Cover design and layout by: **Dynasty Cover Me**
Book interior design by: **Shawn Walker**
Edited by**: Cassandra Sims**

Stay Connected with Us!

Text **LOCKDOWN** to 22828 to stay up-to-date with new releases, sneak peaks, contests and more…
Or **CLICK HERE** to sign up.
Thank you.

Like our page on Facebook:

Lock Down Publications: Facebook

Join Lock Down Publications/The New Era Reading Group

Visit our website @ www.lockdownpublications.com

Follow us on Instagram:

Lock Down Publications: Instagram

Email Us: We want to hear from you!

Submission Guideline.

Submit the first three chapters of your completed manuscript to ldpsubmissions@gmail.com, subject line: Your book's title. The manuscript must be in a .doc file and sent as an attachment. Document should be in Times New Roman, double spaced and in size 12 font. Also, provide your synopsis and full contact information. If sending multiple submissions, they must each be in a separate email.

Have a story but no way to send it electronically? You can still submit to LDP/Ca$h Presents. Send in the first three chapters, written or typed, of your completed manuscript to:

LDP: Submissions Dept
Po Box 870494
Mesquite, Tx 75187

DO NOT send original manuscript. Must be a duplicate.

Provide your synopsis and a cover letter containing your full contact information.

Thanks for considering LDP and Ca$h Presents.

DEDICATION

Dedicated to all the people who continue to motivate me. Special thanks to my wife, children and friends. You all increase my determination to be all I'm capable of being.

PRELUDE

General Chan found himself standing before the High Council. He was nervous, and fear crept up and down his spine. No matter how many times he'd been before them, it always seemed like the first, because he was aware the visit could mean his death. And death seemed more of a realistic thought, seeing the assassins who stood in silence around the wall.

"General Chan, do you know why you've been summoned?"

The general knelt on his right knee before bowing his head.

"Headmaster Hia Xan Tu, the Brown Locusts are seeing to the end of the treacherous Po Clan in America and China. This, I'm sure of."

"That sounds good, General Chan, but there are no fools here. The High Council is not ignorant of the defiance and death your clan has come to experience at the expense of the attempts to make the Po Chan honor our contract. However, we're counting on you to do as you've thought to do."

"May my blood be spilled upon my own blade if I don't, Headmaster Hia Xan Tu."

"So be it, General Chan. Your family is counting on you. Their lives are resting within the balance with your ability to fulfill your Oath.

"I will not let you down."

"Good. This meeting is over. Hopefully, our next meeting shall be to celebrate your success."

"Indeed, it shall, Headmaster Hia Xan Tu."

General Chan stood, bowed, and walked out. Back in his car, he opened the glove compartment and retrieved his cellphone. He scrolled down his list of contacts until he found the one he was searching for. Before making the phone call, he took a moment to gather himself and get his nerves under control. *One day I'll have a seat at the table with the High Council,* he thought, as he touched the icon next to the contact's name. The phone rang twice before the lines were connected. A male's voice came through the speaker of the phone. The two of them went back and forth in Chinese for eight minutes.

Whatever he'd said must've been to General Chan's delight because he smiled. With a clear picture of what was about to happen in America, he thanked his contact in Chinese before ending the call.

CHAPTER ONE

Tabitha Greene and her partner, Jennifer Tinsley, were up bright and early—they had to be to get through Tabitha's yoga and exercise routine before showering and heading to work. In bra and panties, both women transitioned from pose to pose effortlessly. As they moved from forward fold to downward facing dog, the doorbell rang.

“I’ll get it,” Jennifer said. She stood and put on a house coat before going to answer the door. Reaching the door, she peeped through the peephole to see who it was, but there was nobody to be seen. Curiously, she unlocked the door and eased it open to a crack. Still, she didn't see anyone.

Just as she was about to open the door wider, two ninja stars struck and stuck in the outside of the front door. Quickly, Jennifer slammed the door shut and braced herself against the wall. Realizing she hadn’t locked the door back, she did so hurriedly and with shaking hands.

“Tabby, they're here!”

Upon hearing the panic within her voice, Tabitha sprang to her feet and ran to the front door, where she embraced a frightened Jennifer.

“Who's here, Jenn?”

“There are two ninja stars stuck in our front door. If they'd waited a little longer, the stars would've been stuck in me.”

The reality of what she was saying infuriated her. Tabitha held her at arm’s length and stared into her eyes where the fear was unmistakable.

“Jenn, listen to me. I want you to lock yourself in the bathroom. Don't open the door until I knock on it and you hear my voice. Understand?”

She nodded to express her understanding. Before she did as she was told, Jennifer grabbed a navy blue skirt suit. *I might as well take a shower and get dressed for work*, she thought. Safely locked inside of the bathroom, she jumped in the shower.

Tabitha tried to turn the knob of the bathroom door. Seeing it was locked and secure, and hearing the shower, she hurried into the bedroom and over to the walk-in closet. Inside, she opened the secret compartment in the back, behind the hanging clothes, and grabbed the sheathed sword. She slipped on a pair of spandex pants and a halter top, and barefoot, she walked out, and headed for the back door.

She eased the back door open and stepped out into the light of the early morning. The crisp, cool air filled her lungs. She surveyed the area before stepping off the porch, into the open. *Humph, no one in sight. . . but that doesn't mean the assassins are gone,* she contemplated.

As soon as she stepped one foot off the porch, she found herself tucking and rolling right, to evade the oncoming assault of the razor sharp instruments of death. Ending the roll in a kneeling position, she knocked the last ninja star down with the sheathed sword. Two ninjas flipped off the roof, landing on their feet with swords already drawn.

"Guys, do we really have to do this?"

They responded by attacking.

Without drawing her blade, Tabitha blocked and evaded the slashes and thrusts of the swords. She didn't attempt a counterattack because of the speed and proficiency in which the two ninjas used the instruments of death they wielded. They fought with determination to end her life.

One of her attackers tried a thrust maneuver, which she sidestepped, and swept the assassin off his feet with the sheath of her sword. Before she could unsheathe her sword, the other ninja launched an attack, slashing at her with his blade. She did a backdrop to evade, and upon springing back to her feet, she pulled her blade. The steel blades clashed in a malicious dance of death.

After the assassins realized their target was just as skilled as they were, they retreated and changed the focus of their attack, which was a big mistake because it gave Tabitha the break she needed to focus.

With the sword in her left hand and sheath in the other, she welcomed their attack. As the one to her left slashed, she battled his sword down with the sheath, and with a swift spin motion, drove the blade of her sword through his stomach. The weight of the dead corpse slumped over her back confirmed the kill.

Outraged from seeing his comrade felled, the last standing attacker yelled at her in Chinese and attacked. Tabitha sheathed her sword and dropped it on the ground before he reached her. Out of anger, he swung wildly. Making it easy for her to anticipate his every maneuver, she remained just beyond the reach of the blade, timing his motions.

Tabitha slid inside striking distance after catching her opponent off guard with a thrust kick to the stomach, causing him to drop his weapon. Hand-to-hand combat, he was no match for her. She stunned the ninja with a flurry of elbows, from spinning, reverse, to uppercuts elbows. Afterwards, she went into a handstand. Gripping the attacker's head between her legs, she took him down to the ground, where she used the power of her legs to snap his neck with a twist. After the second kill, her adrenaline rush returned.

She refocused before picking up her sword and proceeded to continue checking the area, to make sure there was no more threats to her and Jennifer's livelihood. She stepped out in the open, making herself appear to be an easy target. She figured if there were any in hiding, they would jump on the opportunity. But since no projectiles came flying her way, she concluded within her mind, everything was pretty much back to normal. Tabitha opened the door to the toolshed. She dragged the dead bodies inside and locked the door when she left.

Back inside the house, she calmed herself and put on a heartwarming smile, before knocking on the bathroom door.

"Jenn, you can open the door now."

Jennifer opened the bathroom door. Her body language spoke calmness, but the look in her eyes displayed a reflection of fear and worry. She wrapped her arms around Tabitha and squeezed with all her might.

"Tabby, I love you so much."

Tabitha kissed her on her right cheek.

"Jenn, I know. I love you more. Let me call Saki and Ken to bring them up to speed on what happened."

They walked into the bedroom. Jennifer sat on the side of the bed while Tabitha made the necessary phone calls. After talking to both, Saki and Ken, they informed her of the time they'd be arriving with the clean-up crew. Ending the call, she hung up and turned her full attention back to Jennifer.

"Okay, Jenn, we have thirty minutes before the calvary arrives. That means I have a good twenty minutes to give your body the attention it needs right now. What do you say, luv?"

Jennifer stood to her feet and relieved her body of the clothes that clung to every curve. "Tabby, I suggest we make every second count."

"My thoughts exactly." Tabitha walked up on Jennifer and kissed her passionately while massaging her breasts.

She moaned at the gentleness of her touch.

Playfully, Tabitha pushed her back onto the bed and climbed on top of her, kissing her while roaming, exploring between Jennifer's inner-thighs with her left hand. She gasped for air as Tabitha's fingers entered her sex, stroking slowly.

Feeling the heat and moisture level rising around her fingers, Tabitha removed her fingers from inside of Jennifer and licked them while staring into her glossed over eyes. She then began kissing her way down the center of Jennifer's body, stopping momentarily to kiss, massage, and suck on the erect nipples of her pleasantly pump and expertly tanned breasts.

Jennifer sighed, moaned, and squirmed under her skillful touch. Tabitha knew how to please her in every way knowing she yearned to be pleased. She continued her descent by lightly gliding her tongue down Jennifer's belly, stopping to kiss her navel before descending between her thighs. As her tongue slid up and down the length of the opening to Jennifer's sex, an orgasm quaked throughout Jennifer's body, causing her to tremble and arch her lower back upward.

When Tabitha's tongue entered her, the arch in Jennifer's back deepened before she rolled her hips forward, forcing her tongue deeper inside. Jennifer climaxed again before Tabitha released her from beneath her pleasurable thoughts.

She rolled over onto her back on the bed and lay next to Jennifer, who was flushed and enjoying the euphoric moment. Remembering she had to go to work, Jennifer jumped up and ran to the bathroom to wash up before leaving for work.

On her way out the door, she stopped and kissed Tabitha on the left side of her neck as she began cleaning her sword. Tabitha smiled and kept her focus on what she was doing because she knew one false move or mistake could cause her to be missing a couple fingers. Jennifer hadn't been gone five minutes before Saki and Sia arrived.

They sat inside with Tabitha in casual conversation until Kenneth and Angel showed up. She led the way to the toolshed and unlocked the door so they could enter. Once inside, she turned on the light, revealing the dead assassins bodies, propped up against the interior wall, behind the door.

Saki walked over and knelt beside the corpse on the right. Although the brown ninja suit told her the identity of the Clan, she still had a few questions for Tabitha.

“My sister, Tabitha, what happened?”

Tabitha told them what had happened scene by scene. Kenneth and Sia shared looks of concern. Angel was Angel. She showed no sign of emotion at all, something Tabitha had always found unnerving about her, but at the same time it amazed her, considering she was a woman.

Saki took the right glove off of the hand of the dead body she was kneeling beside. She called Tabitha over to her side. “Tabitha, do you see the markings upon his hand?” Tabitha studied the oddly shaped symbol. Saki realized she was looking at it upside down, and turned the hand to give Tabitha a different angle.

“Yes, Master Saki, I see it. What is it?”

Saki let go of the lifeless hand and stood to her feet. "It is the symbol of the locust. These misguided brothers were members of The Brown Locusts. They serve the High Council. Where is Jennifer now?"

"She went to work. Why?"

"Jennifer's not safe there. We must go to her job in a hurry before it is too late."

Tabitha looked down at the lifeless bodies. "What about this mess?"

"Tabitha, the cleaners shall arrive any moment now. Do not let the dead trouble you. Let's focus on keeping the living whom we love, alive."

Tabitha turned the light off but left the toolshed door unlocked for the clean-up crew, and they left. She rode in the car with Kenneth and Angel, following behind Saki and Sia, who rode together.

They arrived at the federal building's guard outpost. Thankfully, Saki and Tabitha still had clearance, so they made it through the security checks without a problem. With Saki and Sia still in front, they pulled into the inside parking garage. Sia pulled out her iPhone and called Tabitha. She answered on the second ring.

"Hello?"

"Tabitha, it's me, Sia. Pay close attention to the shadows. If they are here, that's where they will be lurking until their target is spotted."

"Okay, Sia. Be safe."

"My exact thoughts to you, Tabitha." They hung up.

Tabitha was about to relay the message to Kenneth and Angel but realized she didn't have to.

"They're here. I can sense their presence. They're moving through the shadows." Angel said, looking around cautiously.

At a slow speed, the two cars cruised around inside the parking garage. Angel didn't feel their presence as strong until they reached the southern wing. Out of her peripheral, she noticed the motion within her blind spots. She told Tabitha to call Sia back and inform her on the whereabouts of the trained killers hiding in the shadows.

Tabitha didn't want to be a messenger, so she hit Sia on speed dial and handed her phone to Angel. She sat back in the backseat with her arms folded and legs crossed. Angel didn't attempt to hide the smirk, but instead of speaking her mind, she took the phone and returned to her forward seated position in the front passenger seat.

Sia answered on the first ring. "Hello? Is there something wrong, Tabitha?"

Angel noticed the affectionate tone of Sia's voice thinking she was talking to Tabitha. It was comical and she was almost tempted to play along, but it wasn't the right time, nor the proper place for the picking.

"Wrong woman, Sia—this is Angel."

"Oops. I apologize, Master Angel."

"No offense taken. Listen, they're all hiding in the shadows in the southern wing. We should park in the east wing and travel by foot back over."

"Okay, Master Angel. I'll inform Master Saki immediately."

Angel could hear the two women conversing on the other end in Chinese, and since she herself spoke Chinese fluently, she knew exactly what was being said, and what had been concluded, before Sia's voice came back through the phone speaking in broken English.

"We'll park in the east wing and talk strategy before we walk to the south wing."

"Alright, Sia. Anything you'd like me to tell Tab before I hang up?"

Sia giggled and hung up without responding. To Angel, the giggle said it all.

They cruised over to the far end of the east wing and parked right next to each other and got out. Saki approached Angel and bowed before speaking.

"Master Angel, how many Brown Locusts are there in the southern wing?"

"Master Saki, I counted six. Neither really skilled in the dark acts."

Saki nodded. "I see. So, what strategy do you propose, Master Angel?"

“Do as your training inspires you to do. Malice and I will travel through the shadows. We are in a federal parking garage, so the quicker and quieter, the better.”

“Agreed. Let’s get this over with. Master Sia and Tabitha, come with me.”

Saki, Tabitha, and Sia began walking casually out in the open, down the eastern wing. Angel reached inside her overcoat inner pocket and pulled out a green, silk satchel. Before they silently took to the shadows, she opened it and handed Malice three of the seven ninja stars concealed inside of it. Although Saki, Sia, and Tabitha were in their sights, Malice and Angel paid them little to no attention since their focus was in the shadows.

As they entered the southern wing, Sia closed the space between her and Tabitha, as if she felt the need to shield her. They followed closely behind Saki, who stopped and stood dead center of the south wing of the parking garage. The three women stood back to back. Facing the shadows as they came to life, four of the six Brown Locusts came flipping out and surrounded them.

Before the assassins could launch their attack, the silent stars of death whispered upon the still air and cut them down. Seeing their targets grounded, Malice and Angel stepped out of the shadows and approached Saki, Sia, and Tabitha.

Displaying a smile, Saki bowed and spoke. “Very quickly and quietly, Master Angel. I would ask the whereabouts of the other two but that would be a senseless question. Our job is done here.” She turned her attention to Tabitha. “Be sure to send Jennifer a text telling her to make haste straight to the restaurant upon leaving work. It's nonnegotiable.”

Instead of replying, Tabitha took her cellphone out and did as she'd been instructed. Moments afterwards, she received an incoming text from Jennifer with the thumbs up emoji. “She said okay. Now, what are we going to do about these dead bodies?”

Malice walked over to the nearest lifeless body, grabbed it by the right ankle, and dragged it over to the shadows. After repeating his actions on the remaining three bodies, he looked to Sia, his eyes narrowed, and eyebrows furrowed. But, before she could answer the questioning expression, she dove forward sideways, twisting her body in the air while catching the blow dart with the forefinger and middle finger of her right hand, as she landed in a kneeling position. And without looking in the direction it had come from, she released the dart in rapid succession, and with lightning speed the dart took flight spinning in a 360◦ motion, flying back into the shadows.

The faint sound of a body hitting the concrete floor of the garage caused everyone to focus on Sia's outstretched arm, pointed in the direction the sound had come from.

Saki and Malice rushed towards the shadowy spot and returned dragging, a barely breathing, Brown Locust. While the two held the assassin down, Sia removed the mask, revealing the face of a young Chinese lady who didn't look to be older than twenty years old.

Immediately, Sia began to interrogate the young woman in their native tongue. As the two women conversed, the young assassin spoke harshly, but quickly softened her tone once she realized Sia meant her no harm. Because they were competent in the Chinese dialogue, Saki, Malice, and Angel listened intently. Tabitha, on the other hand, disregarded the conversation and kept watch due to the possibility of surprise attacks, or Federal officials.

After the Brown Locust had given Sia all the information she sought to gain, she asked Sia to put an end to her suffering. Sia unsheathed one of the Locust Daggers from the Brown Locust's person and drove the blade through the right side of her neck, severing a main artery. The young assassin's eyes locked in the death stare, looking into Sia's eyes. She snatched the blade out and placed it back in the sheath and let it rest on the Brown Locust's lap. She stood up straight and sighed before addressing Saki, Malice, Angel, and Tabitha.

"This was a decoy. They wouldn't have harmed a hair on Jennifer's head. Their only reasoning for coming here was in hopes of getting the exact reaction we gave them. Masters Malice and

Angel, we must hurry to the Guild—that's where the real strike force is waiting in the shadows to strike."

Malice dragged the corpse into the shadows where he'd hidden the others before they walked back to the far end of the eastern wing of the parking garage. Saki and Sia got back in her gloss black Mercedes Jeep. Malice and Angel, along with Tabitha in the backseat, hopped inside his Audi 8 and sped out of the parking garage at the speed limit.

Once out of the federal jurisdiction, Malice led the way doing ninety five as they made their way to The Slaughter House.

***

General Chan, along with four of his personal guards, stood at the entrance of the Sune Compound, which was home to the Sune Clan, better known as The Green Mantis. They'd been waiting for several minutes for a welcoming escort who came after another ten minutes of silence.

A young Chinese girl standing about four feet five inches tall with hair that reached the small of her back entered the room surrounded by seven Green Mantises.

General Chan bowed to the young girl, who didn't appear to be more than fourteen years old. With a blank expression on her face, she returned the honorable gesture and greeting before speaking.

"General Chan, I am Yishi Pe Sune. Daughter of Master Ma Sune. Welcome to our home. Follow me."

With her guards surrounding her, she turned around and began walking. Not wanting to get too close, General Chan and the four Brown Locusts followed a few paces behind, fearing the Green Mantises might take it as a threat. He knew he nor his guards were a match for them. There was only one clan who could stand toe to toe with the Green Mantises, and that was the Po Clan, better known as the Black Dragons.

Upon entering the main area of the compound, General Chan immediately noticed the changes that had been made. The Green Mantis symbol had been engraved within the door posts of every building and the green flag on top of each building moved with the flow of the wind.

Yishi Pe Sune stopped out front of a fairly large building and turned around to speak to General Chan. “My mother, Master Ma Sune, is expecting you. Your personal guards are to remain outside.” With her right hand, Yishi Pe Sune gestured for him to enter the building. General Chan was a little hesitant at first and Yishi sensed it.

“General Chan, this is my mother's study. No personal guards are allowed inside. It would be disrespectful to consider war in such a peaceful place. Besides, if that were the case, Master Ma Sune could handle you by herself.”

The general chuckled, nervous at the mention of an undeniable fact. *It's senseless to think one is protected inside of a fortress full of breathing, highly-skilled warriors,* he thought to himself before entering the door.

Once inside, his eyes landed on Ma Sune sitting on a fluffy pillow in a high backless chair, in full lotus. He bowed out of respectful habit, but also because he knew not to assume she wasn't looking at him just because her eyes were closed. When he lifted his gaze, he found himself staring into her dark brown eyes.

She carefully examined the short, pudgy man's body posture before speaking. “General Chan, what brings you here at this hour?”

He studied her just as she'd studied him. An even five feet, her nicely-shaped figure and long, black, silky hair displayed a well-established beauty for a woman of forty-three. Unlike most of the clans, the Sune forbade the marking of their body, so in his mind she was flawless.

“General Chan?”

Hearing Ma Sune call his name broke him out of the fantasy that had slowly started building in his mind. “Forgive my absentmindedness, Master Ma Sune.”

“Time isn't precious, however, the cosmic orbit is. In other words, General Chan, I don't have all day. State your affairs, so we can come to terms with a resolution, and you can be on your way." She spoke with a stern expression, void of emotion.

General Chan wasn't accustomed to women talking to him with such authority, but Ma Sune wasn't an ordinary woman. There was a legend about her in Beijing, China—a legend he wasn't trying to be on the unfortunate side of. He chose his words carefully, masking his dislike for her superior tone of voice.

"Master Ma Sune, I assure you I'm not here on a fool's errand. I have news of importance that you might find an interest in."

"I'm listening."

"I've sent Brown Locusts to America to seek out the Po Clan hiding there, and I've given orders to eliminate them. I received word back from one of my men, and I was informed that Saki Po is the new head of the traitors."

"Saki Po. . . Why does the name sound so familiar?"

"Master Ma Sune, Saki Po is the daughter of Khia Li Po and Han Xi Po, the two masters who started the Po Clan's rebellion against the High Council."

"Hmm. . . Interesting. Continue, General Chan."

He took her interest as an invitation to take a seat in the chair in front of the green and black, swirl-marble desk. What he didn't know was, Ma Sune's left hand was on the handle of her sword, and she was debating if she should slit his throat, or not. With no clue that he was in danger, he proceeded to get comfortable and continued to relay the information.

"So, after I received the information concerning Saki Po, I had a couple officers do some research. Come to find out her little brother Qi Dom Po lived in the open, not in hiding. I had my guys arrest him on trumped up charges."

Ma Sune's hand jerked on the handle of her sword. It took every bit of will power she had to hold her composure. It was obvious to her; General Chan didn't know Khia Li Po's maiden name was Khia Li Sune. She was one of the three triplets, Ma, Khia and Shuri. She had heard enough, and the plan had already taken form in her mind.

"General Chan, you've surely stated things that interest me. Hopefully, no harm has come to Qi Dom Po. If so, you do realize the Black Dragon will not stop until all parties involved in harming him are dead, and that includes their family as well."

General Chan hadn't thought about that, and Ma Sune could tell by his facial expression.

"Is the young man safe, General Chan?"

"Well, Master Ma Sune, as far as I know he is. How about I release him into your custody, and let you hold him as your prisoner? I'll send a few of my men to have him brought here before the moon is over."

"No, General Chan. I'll send a couple of my people with you, and they will bring him here," Ma Sune replied. She forced herself to let go of the hilt of her sword before she stood to her feet.

"Now, General Chan, if that is all you came for, I suggest you be on your way. Men do have a knack to get into fights in jail. Try pleading such a case before a Black Dragon concerning their leader's brother."

In his mind, the picture she painted was very plain and full of wisdom. Nervously, General Chan stood and bowed. "Understood, Master Ma Sune, I'll be on my way. We'll wait on your people at the entrance."

"My people will be waiting on you to make it to the front gates, General Chan. Hopefully, our next meeting will be more pleasant."

"Indeed." He bowed again before leaving.

Once the doors closed again, two assassins dressed in forest green ninja suits came out of the shadows within the room. Ma Sune nodded, and they left. *What is already understood needs no verbal instructions,* she thought.

***

Malice, Angel, Tabitha, Saki, and Sia arrived at the slaughterhouse. They sat in their cars in the parking lot scoping out the scene. Malice had called Trent and told him what was going on and to be on point. His phone vibrated on the dashboard.

"Hello?"

"Master Malice, although it doesn't seem like it, we are surrounded. We will divert their attention while you and Angel get inside. We shall join you all shortly. Tell Tabitha she knows what to do."

Saki hung up the phone without waiting for a reply. Angel looked at Malice as he tossed his phone back on the dashboard. Before she could ask, he was already answering her question.

"That was Saki informing us that we are surrounded. Angel, you and I are to make a run for it while they divert their attention. Tabitha, Saki said you know what to do."

"Of course, become a target so the prince and his princess can run to safety," she answered sarcastically.

Angel turned around in the front seat to face her. "Tab, I'm about sick of your funky little attitude for the day."

"It's called sarcasm, Angel."

Tabitha stretched her hands out towards Angel. "Stars please."

Angel handed her three ninja stars. "Make them count, Tab."

"I plan on it, Angel. You two wait until I say go."

Before she could open the rear passenger side door up, the assault began. Three ninja stars stuck inside the exterior back door. Tabitha took a deep breath, pushed the door wide open, and rolled to her right quickly. Her quick actions were just in time to evade the silent, razor-sharp stars of death. Instead, they ended up sticking into the backseat where she'd been sitting just seconds prior. By the time she was back on her feet, she found herself rolling left to avoid another series of stars that had been maliciously thrown her way.

Seeing the path of the assault, Saki and Sia opened the car doors and dove out of their seats sideways. In a kneeling position, they waited, knowing it wouldn't be long before they became the focus of the assault. Once the projectiles started flying their way, they took action. One by one, they picked the Brown Locusts off with a series of ninja stars.

Tabitha was still facing heavy fire. The instruments of death lay on the asphalt all about her. Tired of taking the defensive roll, she rolled right and came up on her right knee before throwing two stars at once, bringing death to two of their enemies. "Now!" she yelled, looking over her shoulder at Angel, who seemed to be admiring her skills.

Without hesitation, Malice and Angel pushed the front doors of the Audi 8 open and ran inside the building. Saki and Sia made their way over to Tabitha. And together, they caused death's presence to be felt and feared causing The Brown Locusts to retreat.

Casually, and as if nothing of the sort had taken place, Saki, Sia, and Tabitha walked into the slaughterhouse.

Malice told the customers they were closing for the remainder of the week. They paid for the packaged meats and left. Afterwards, the customers were gone, he gathered everyone inside the training room. He left the doors open, so he could hear if anyone entered the building while they discussed their options.

"Master Saki, what's the estimated count for those still alive?"

"Master Malice, twelve at the most. None when we're done here, but that doesn't account for those who aren't here. It's not safe here."

"What do you suggest we do, Master Saki?"

"Gather everything of importance and return to this room. Those of your guild who are not known should just leave now and go home. The rest shall come with us to the restaurant."

Malice took her advice. After they gathered weapons and other valuables, the members of the guild met back up in the training room, where Saki, Sia, and Tabitha sat in silence. And after the unknown members of the guild left, the only members remaining were Malice, Angel, and Trent. They carried two duffle bags each. Just as Malice opened his mouth to speak, Sia held her finger against her lips to silence him. She pointed up towards the ceiling.

Angel heard the faint sound of feet shuffling. *Why would they be on the roof?* Her forehead wrinkled and her lips twisted to one side as a frown grew over her face. She contemplated silently before it donned on her. "Everybody, out! Now," she shouted. No one questioned her, instead, they hurried out of the room. And, just as she'd figured, an explosion came and a loud *boom!* sounded throughout the interior of the space, causing the walls to shake before the ceiling of the training room caved in. Saki's estimate had been right on the money. Twenty Brown Locusts fell through the hole of the roof, crashing down on top of the debris.

Malice, Angel, and Trent dropped the bags. Trent opened one of the duffle bags he carried and took out six swords and handed one to Saki, Sia, Malice, and Angel. He tried to give one to Tabitha, but she declined and asked if he had two short handled sickles. Just so happened he did so, he handed her the weapons of choice from one of the other duffle bags.

Next, he unsheathed the two swords and readied himself for the oncoming attack. Saki, Sia, Angel, and Tabitha didn't wait on the Brown Locusts to come to them, instead, they walked fearlessly into battle with Malice and Trent bringing up the rear.

The four fearless women felled ten of the assassins before they changed their method of attack. With Malice and Trent felling three on arrival, the Brown Locusts were down to seven. Well, five after Tabitha ended two more of their lives with a 360° whirlwind attack. The razor-sharp blades and fine points of the sickles dug and sliced through the throats of her targets like a knife cutting through butter.

Sia found herself in a real sword fight with two of the remaining assassins. Her sword clashed with theirs as she twisted and turned, evading the blade when she didn't have time to block. Both assassins attempted a downward slashing move at the same time. She blocked both blades and sprang into the air, taking them both down with a single roundhouse heel kick.

The two assassins hit the floor dazed. Before they could get it together, Trent fell upon them, thrusting the blades through their chests. Angel had dropped her sword purposely. She beckoned with her right hand for the three ninjas to attempt an attack and they obliged her. Then she allowed the three Brown Locusts to surround her. She closed her eyes and kept them closed. Her actions infuriated the three and their anger ushered them into an attack—an attack that caused them their lives.

When the first three swung, Angel side stepped the thrusting blade and spun around to stand behind the attacker. Before the assassin could turn around, she snapped his neck. The other two leapt at her with their swords pointing at her like spears. She back dropped, allowing them to land behind her. But by the time they landed, she had sprang back to her feet. When the two Brown Locusts spun around to face her, she hit them both with open palm strikes in the solar plexus simultaneously. Blood spewed from their mouths upon contact, and they fell dead.

Angel opened her eyes and took a deep breath before speaking. "Okay, Tabitha, you must remain calm and free of any emotion until we have completed our tasks and returned to our physical bodies. Understood?"

Not use to what was going on, Tabitha nodded in the affirmative. As Angel stretched her left arm out before her, an ethereal sword materialized within her hand. Her actions brought great interest to Tabitha.

"This is the ultimate reality, Tabitha. Here, it's about will and being able to wield your will into the object needed. Focus your energies, and your weapon of choice will always be within your immediate grasp."

Tabitha focused like never before and stretched both arms out in front of her, and shorthanded sickles materialized in both hands. "Now what?" she asked curiously.

"Now, we hunt. Let's travel around to see if any of the enemies are about. Follow me, Tabitha, and remember, no emotion."

"Oh, believe me, I'll remember. Lead the way, Angel."

Side by side, Angel and Tabitha walked straight through the wall into the light of day. Angel led the way around the building, looking around for any suspicious movements or activity. Then the memory of how she'd felt, and her vision when she first partook in a mission to bring absolute death, hit her, and she stopped. Facing Tabitha, she asked, "What is it you see?"

"Imagine a person's vision while hallucinating on shrooms. A bunch of colors keep exploding and making new colors."

"I figured that. This calls for a slight change of focus. Think of the world as you're used to seeing it. You know how things look around the restaurant, right?"

Tabitha followed Angel's instructions to the tee, and everything began to look normal around her.

"Thank you, Angel. Now I can see buildings, vehicles, and people again."

"Great. Let's continue to look around." They circled the perimeter of the restaurant twice. Reason being, Angel wanted Tabitha to get a feel of what she called, *reality*. Back at the point they started, they stopped.

"Well, Tabitha, there seems to be no threats on the ground level. The only place left to check is the roof."

Tabitha looked up. The roof was a good forty feet up. She looked back at Angel questioningly.

"Tabitha, the beauty about eternity is there are no limitations. Again, the will to do is what gets done." Angel began to levitate. Loving a challenge, Tabitha focused her thoughts on doing the same, and likewise, she also started to levitate. The two women, in their astral body, ascended to the top of the roof of the restaurant. And, just as Angel had thought, fifteen Brown Locusts were crouched down near the ledge of the roof, waiting for the perfect opportunity to attack.

"The great part about all of this is they can't hear or see us, Tabitha. However, let's give you your first true killing experience. You take the seven on the left, and I got the seven on the right. We'll see who gets that eighth kill of the day."

"So, what do I do, Angel?"

"Run your blade right through them. There won't be a bone or flesh that can stop you. I promise. Now, shall we?"

Tabitha responded by starting the death toll. Her ethereal sickles snatched the spirit out of the bodies of her enemies. And as one sickle severed the spirit from their bodies and souls, the other sickle cut the spirit asunder. It was new to her, but she was proving to be effective at it.

Angel, on the other hand, let Tabitha get three kills ahead before she launched her attack. In the blink of an eye, she had dispirited the seven on the right with one move. She twisted through the air like a drill, with the sword held straight out and the point of the sword first, her astral form passed through the assassin's body, removing and destroying the spirit along the way. She and Tabitha met up at the eighth kill, and together they ripped the spirit up out of the Brown Locust.

"That's that, Tabitha."

Tabitha was a little confused. The assassins were dead but there was no blood or tears in their clothing to show any sign of the blades entrance.

"Angel where's the blood?"

"This way of killing isn't as messy as the way you're accustomed to, Tabitha. Let's return to our bodies before we're discovered. Besides, the longer we're out here, the more strain on the physical body. We'll need some serious rest when we get back."

The two of them unwielded their weapons before leaping off the top of the roof. They walked back through the wall to enter the basement, where they reentered their bodies. Upon sitting up, the first person Angel took notice of was Saki, who sat in a calm state on the floor. She helped Tabitha to her feet before bowing towards Saki.

"So, where are you two returning from, Master Angel?" Saki questioned, as she spoke her peace.

"A short distance. We did a perimeter check and found fifteen Brown Locusts lying in wait on the roof. All of whom are truly dead. I gotta give it to Tabitha, she's a natural." Saki looked at Tabitha, who looked drained of energy but still managed to bow.

"Master Angel, and Tabitha, go lie down and get some rest. When you wake up, maybe one of you would care to explain the fifteen lifeless corpses on top of the roof."

Tired, Angel and Tabitha walked off, leaving Saki down in the basement. Saki walked back upstairs and told Sia, Trent, Malice, and five members of the Po Clan to come with her. She led the way up on to the roof, where everyone immediately noticed the fifteen dead corpses.

She turned around to face her companions. “If you’re all wondering what happened here, I'll leave that truth to Master Angel or Tabitha to tell. I called you up here to see this for several reasons. Reasons I'm going to make sure are understood when Master Angel and Tabitha awaken from their rest.”

Saki bowed before walking back down the stairs which led directly into the restaurant from the roof. Sia and the other members of the Po Clan followed her down, leaving Trent and Malice on the roof enjoying the air.

“So, Malice, what's the deal with Angel?” Trent probed, bringing up a subject that had been on his mind.

“Bro, she's been putting the press on about getting married.”

“And you said no?”

“I'm Malice. My name isn't suicide or stupid.”

Trent stared at the bodies of the Brown Locusts. “Yeah, you got a point. Any woman capable of doing this isn't a woman to be telling no.”

“They don't call her Angel for nothing, Trent.”

The two men enjoyed the fresh air in silence for a few more minutes before heading back down into the restaurant.

CHAPTER TWO

Ma Sune sat in her study. It was midnight, so she was dressed in a forest green night gown. She sipped on a cup of tea while reading a scroll about the history of her clan and the Po Clan. It was entitled *Blood Oath.*

A knock came at the door. Ma Sune knew it could only be for what she'd been up waiting for all night. Speaking in the Chinese dialect, she told them to enter. And in walked two of the Green Mantises with a blindfolded young man in between them.

She instructed one of the assassins to remove the blindfold. After the blindfold had been removed, she dismissed the two Green Mantises. The young man stood still while she looked him over. Qi Dom Po was dark brown and five foot six with silky black hair, neatly trimmed.

"Are you Qi Dom Po, the son of Khia Li Sune Po and Han Xi Po?"

The lighting in the room was dim, however, after being blindfolded for so long, it still hurt his eyes. Although he couldn't see her, the woman's voice reminded him of someone he hadn't seen in years. He was twenty-three now and the last time he'd heard or seen her he was just seven years of age.

"Are you Qi Dom Po or not? I mean you no harm. We are family."

It was in that moment his eyes finally adjusted and he was able to see the woman standing before him. Qi Dom Po was so happy, he threw his arms around her and hugged her.

"Aunt Ma Sune, am I ever glad to see you." Ma Sune hugged him back.

"Everything is okay. You're safe now." She held him at arm's length. "Now get control of yourself. I understand you're use to the ways of the Po Clan, Qi Dom Po, but now you're on the Sune Clan's compound. Here, the show of emotions is looked at as a sign of deceit and weakness. Do you understand?"

Qi Dom Po straightened up, put on a serious facial expression to match Ma Sune's, and bowed. “Yes ma'am, understood, and forgive me for my ignorance, Aunt Ma Sune.”

“Forgiven. Just remember what you've just learned about our side of your blood and you'll fit right in.”

She and her nephew talked for an hour before she escorted him to his sleeping quarters which he found to his delight.

“Get a good bath and some rest. After the morning rituals and meal, I'll call a meeting for you to meet everyone.”

“Alright, Aunt Ma Sune. Good night.” He bowed, and she returned the greeting before leaving him to bathe and rest.

By the time Qi Dom Po finished bathing, the first thing he noticed was the change of attire laying across the bed. He moved the clothes to the back of the chair, which set in the far right corner of the room, and jumped in the bed. Sleep claimed his tired body as soon as his head touched the soft plush pillow.

***

The flow of business inside the Po Clan's restaurant was great. The place was nearly filled to the capacity. Businessmen were having business meetings, couples were on dates, and singles were completing reposts on iPads, while enjoying their meals and beverages. Sia and Malice worked the cash register, Saki and Trent helped in the kitchen, and Angel and Tabitha were still resting.

Malice could tell Sia was in deep thought by the way she handled the exchange of currency whenever change was needed for a customer. To be four foot six, Sia's dark brown skin and petite body radiated with energy that grabbed his attention. After the payments for orders came to an end, he decided to pry and probe her thoughts a little.

“Master Sia, is everything alright? You haven't been your usual upbeat self lately.”

She forced a weak smile, hoping he would take the hint, but it didn't work.

“Master Sia?”

"Master Malice, if you must know, I've had a lot on my mind lately. Actually, my concern is for Tabitha. I'm extremely attached to her so to speak."

"Aren't we all?" he replied in a nonchalant manner, as if he wasn't aware of what Sia really meant. They continued to talk while the opportunity presented itself. He noticed, the more they talked about his cousin, the lighter Sia's mood got. She was in the middle of a sentence when she looked up and saw Jennifer walking towards them.

Instead of completing the sentence, when Jennifer sat on the stool closest to where they stood behind the bar, Sia dropped the conversation altogether. Jennifer didn't hesitate in starting a conversation.

"What's up, Sia?"

Sia nodded. Not feeling up to the task of entertaining, she excused herself to see if Saki needed any help in the kitchen. Jennifer frowned at her sudden departure. She watched until Sia was no longer in sight before she addressed Malice.

"Ken, what's up with Sia? She isn't her normal self today."

"I guess she's got a lot on her plate, Jenn. How are you doing though?"

"Great, but starving. I'll take today's special."

"Coming right up."

Malice looked over his left shoulder and yelled Jennifer's order to the back in Chinese. Two minutes later, Saki came casually walking to the front carrying the order. She sat the tray on the counter and placed the order right in front of her.

"How you doing, Jennifer? Tabitha's resting right now. Even when she does wake up, she won't be available for another hour or so. Enjoy your meal."

Since all of her questions had been answered before she even asked, Jennifer held her peace and went to work on the stir-fried brown rice, cabbage, peppers and onions and meatless chicken smothered in honey mustard soy sauce.

Saki turned her attention to Malice. "Master Malice, it's five minutes before closing time. Sia and everyone else are already waiting in the basement. We will close up before joining them. Hopefully, our two traveling spirits will be up by the time we're done."

"Double trouble is already up."

Saki and Jennifer followed his gaze. Coming up the stairs that led to the sleeping quarters were Angel and Tabitha. Jennifer stopped eating, got up, and ran into Tabitha's embrace.

Angel was annoyed by her giddiness, so she walked on over to Malice and kissed him on the cheek before speaking. "Hi, handsome. How're you feeling after a day of hard labor?"

"Thanks for the kiss, Angel, but that's not gonna get you and Tab out of the frying pan. Matter of fact, I'm glad to see you two troublemakers are up and about. You can help me, and Master Saki close up so we can get this meeting over with."

"Why do I feel like me and Tab just got hit with double jeopardy?"

Malice hunched his shoulders. "Don't know, Angel. Ask Master Saki, she's standing right behind you." He walked off and began the process of closing the restaurant, leaving Angel and Saki to talk.

Angel did an about face and bowed.

Saki returned the greeting before speaking. "Master Angel, no one ever said you two were wrong for your actions. However, it would've been wise to inform someone of your actions, so your physical bodies would've been guarded."

"Your constructive criticism is greatly understood, Master Saki."

The two of them began helping Malice close up. Jennifer and Tabitha stood near the stairs to the sleeping quarters talking. Tabitha could tell Jennifer was tired and needed rest.

"Jenn, you look tired. Are you okay?"

"Let's see. I've had ninjas try to kill me. Other than that, I'm okay, but I guess I am a little tired."

Tabitha grabbed her by the hand and led her down the stairs and into their room. Jennifer took one look at the queen size bed and smiled. She was about to dive on to it when Tabitha stopped her.

"I think not. I grabbed some clothes and things from the house so we could shower and get comfortable. Look through the bags over there in the corner. Besides, I need my wifey fresh, clean, and rested by the time I get back."

Jennifer responded by kissing her on the lips.

Tabitha waited until she was in the shower before trotting back up the stairs. She picked up the remaining dirty dishes and carried them to the dishwasher and waited in silence for the wash and rinse cycles to finish.

While waiting, her thoughts went back to the day's events. In less than twenty-four hours, she'd killed and seen more death than she had in her twenty-three years of living. The buzz of the machine snapped her out of memory lane. She helped dry the dishes by towel while Angel and Malice stacked and stored the dishes. With the dishes done and front door locked, Saki flipped the light switch off. They made their way down to the basement where everyone had been patiently waiting their arrival.

Malice took a seat between Trent and an elderly woman of the Po Clan. Saki motioned for Angel and Tabitha to join her up front, standing before everyone. As soon as they took center stage, the casual conversation that was going around ceased, and everyone's attention was on them.

Saki bowed before addressing the people. "Greetings. I know we've all had a long day— some more laborious than others." She looked at Tabitha and Angel out of her peripheral.

"So, I promise not to keep you here long. I'm going to allow Master Angel, and Tabitha here, to explain how fifteen Brown Locusts ended up dead on top of the roof. Master Angel. Tabitha. The floor is all yours."

Saki walked over to the empty seat next to Sia and sat. Tabitha looked at Angel with pleading eyes.

Angel sighed, knowing she hadn't a clue on what to say or how to explain it, so she addressed their spectators. "Greetings, friends, allies and family. What happened this day was the esoteric arts of the way of ninja. I, myself, am an atheist, meaning, I don't believe in any man-made concepts of a God or Gods, and their way of interacting with their creations.

There are those of us who are only warriors or ninja in body and mind, who only understand the skill to cause death or transformation, to be exact to the physical body. Then, there are us, like me and—" she looked Tabitha in the eyes before continuing her speech, "Tabitha, who are warriors and ninja in spirit, mind and body who understands the skills to cause death to the spirit and body. Or, to best be stated, absolute death. And that's what happened this day. We did what we thought to necessary for the safety of our friends, allies, and family."

Angel bowed and so did Tabitha. Everyone stood to their feet in silence and returned the bow. Sia joined Angel and Tabitha before the Po Clan and guild members and spoke her peace.

"Let what has happened here be remembered. We must train harder to keep our spiritual focus while in combat, because some of the masters of our enemies know this art as well. Rest well because tomorrow we shall train after the completion of our personal and collective duties." Sia bowed. You are all dismissed." Everyone bowed in return before heading for a shower or bath and then bed.

As soon as they entered their room and closed the door, Angel and Malice began kissing and undressing each other. They left a trail of clothes that led to the shower, where they made love under the steaming hot water.

After reaching their climax twice, they showered and went straight to sleep.

***

General Chan was at the station early. We hadn't heard back from the Brown Locusts he'd sent to do his bidding, which could only mean they had failed and were dead. The thought alone angered him. He continued to read over reports and stamped closed files while thinking of what to do next concerning his enemies. After stamping the last closed file, he picked up his cell phone and placed a call.

The phone rang twice before it was answered by a feminine voice. "Li Chang speaking."

“Master Li Chang, this is General Chan.”

“Yes, of course. How might I be of assistance to you General?”

“The Po Clan and their allies in the United States have proven to be stronger than I initially believed them to be.”

“What are you proposing, General?”

General Chan thought for a moment. Although Li Chang was of the same clan, they were divided on their views of how the clan would be best governed.

“Go to New Jersey. Your travel expenses will be paid for, and there will be a handsome reward after you've done what must be done. Are you interested?”

“Why wouldn't I be, General?”

“Great. I'll send over a few from the clan to go with you.”

“No need, I'll take my chances with my own. Besides, I don't need morality getting in the way of reality. Just provide passports and visas for the names. I'll text you the information when we're ready.”

General Chan was about to comment when the line went dead. He sat his phone back on the desk next to a stack of files. Officers and other staff members had come in with cups of coffee and tea. Some looked hungover, as if they’d had a long night. With a bow, he greeted every member who passed him.

***

The sun had begun shining on the horizon. Qi Dom Po had just finished washing his face when he heard his aunt's voice.

“Qi Dom Po, it's time for the morning ritual.”

“On the way out now, Aunt Ma!”

“Stop yelling. I'm not deaf.”

Qi Dom Po came out of the bathroom dressed in the loosely fitting forest green linen pants and shirt. He bowed before Ma Sune.

“I apologize for yelling, Aunt Ma Sune. I'm ready now.” She simply nodded. More so out of the approval of the seamstress’s work, and the fact that the linen and color fitted her nephew well, than the acceptance of his apology.

"Remember what I told you, Qi Dom Po. Show no emotions. Not that we don't have emotions. It's about staying in control of them. Understood?"

"Yes, Ma'am."

"Good. Let's go. I'm sure you won't have any problem going through the morning ritual."

Qi Dom Po and Ma Sune walked and talked as she led the way to the courtyard. She explained to him the custom they kept to by being silent during the morning hours until after the morning meal was over. He listened attentively, not wanting to disrespect or break any of the Sune Clan laws.

"You will get to meet everyone at the morning meal." Ma Sune stopped in midstride and faced him. "Well, not everyone. Some of our family members have dedicated their lives to living in the shadows to better protect this family."

Qi Dom Po caught a glimpse of something moving fast on the rooftop of a building to his right. He looked up to see several ninjas in forest green suits crouching on the ledge.

Ma Sune followed his gaze until her eyes caught sight of them before turning her attention back to him. "Qi Dom Po, never fall for the illusion presented by the ninja."

"What do you mean illusion? They're right there on the ledge of the roof."

"Exactly, however, the way of the ninja is to show you what they want you to see, but you will never see coming your death coming. Show yourselves," she said in her native tongue.

What he saw next caused Qi Dom Po's eyes to open wide. It was as if the assassins had appeared out of thin air. She thanked them in Chinese before bowing, and they bowed silently and hurried off.

"Another lesson to remember, Qi Dom Po." She pushed the tall double doors that opened into the courtyard. Rows upon rows of men, women, and children of all ages sat quietly on mats in meditation. Qi Dom Po noticed an unoccupied mat near a young man about his height and looked to be his age. He took a seat in the lotus like everyone else. He didn't stay sitting long, because when

Ma Sune reached the front everyone stood and bowed. She returned the bow before turning her back to them, facing east.

The morning ritual had begun, which was the meditation art of Tai Chi. Like Ma Sune had said, Qi Dom Po had no problems. He flowed through the motion with ease, feeling and respecting the energy flowing through and around him. It lasted for two hours.

At first, Qi Dom Po thought he was going to be exhausted, but after it was over, he was more energized than he'd been when he started. Still in silence, everyone bowed and left the courtyard to go freshen up for the morning meal. Knowing he didn't know his way around the compound, Ma Sune escorted her nephew back to his sleeping quarters and told him she would be back to get him in half an hour.

She went to her room to freshen up. As she was drying off and toweling her hair dry, her cellphone started ringing. She started not to answer it but seeing the name on the caller ID changed her mind. *It's always good to know your enemies next move*, she thought before answering the call.

"General Chan, I hope this call is very informative since I haven't had time to partake in my morning meal as of yet." Although Ma Sune's commanding tone never ceased to annoy him, he never let it be known because feared her and needed her support.

"Master Ma Sune, I do apologize, however, I do have great news. I've summoned Master Li Chang to end the rebellion of the Po Clan and guild in America. She and Master Xan Khan shall lead the Brown Locusts to victory once and for all.

Ma Sune knew exactly who Li Chang and Xan Khan were. Two Brown Locust masters of the dark arts. She was thinking of a way to warn her niece before the destruction.

"General Chan, I see you've chosen to employ some of those who deal in the darkness. How much financial support do you need from me?"

"None at the moment. I'm working on getting their passports and visas right now. Hopefully, everything will be confirmed by morning. Regardless, they'll be on their flight by tomorrow's moon."

"Well, if you're looking for an opportunity to unite with the Sune Clan, let's hope Master Li Chang and Master Xan Khan get the job done. Until then, keep me informed on the progress, General Chan."

Ma Sune hung up the phone and tossed it on the bed. She got dressed and walked out of her room over to Qi Dom Po's. Together, they walked out into the fresh crisp air, over to the dining hall, where everyone was already seated, waiting on the morning meal to be served. Ma Sune seated Qi Dom Po to her left opposite her daughter, Yishi Pe Sune.

Three minutes after their arrival, the food was brought in by the cooks. They platters of baked, fried, roasted, and steamed salmon, steamed brown rice, crab cakes, and containers of raw honey on the table. The kitchen help followed behind them, serving the meal. No one touched the food before them until every plate had been fixed and the cooks and kitchen help were seated. After the cooks and kitchen help took their seats, the feasting began.

Qi Dom Po didn't play with his food. The taste of the raw honey mixed with the salmon, rice and crab cakes was so delicious, he closed his eyes savoring each bite. He felt someone watching him and looked up to see an elderly woman with long graying hair, sitting at the end of the table, staring at him. Her emotionless stare held his gaze until his mouth began to get watery demanding to be filled with more of the great tasting food.

After everyone had eaten their share, the table was cleared. Still everyone remained silent until the cooks and kitchen help returned.

It was Ma Sune who broke the silence. "We rejoice in making it through another moon. And now I shall give you much more to rejoice for. Qi Dom Po, please stand."

He stood to his feet and bowed. All eyes were fixated upon him and stayed staring at him as Ma Sune continued speaking.

"Qi Dom Po is the son of Master Khia Li Sune Po and Hen Xi Po. Master Khia Li Sune is my twin sister."

She looked over at her other sister Wya Mi Sune. "Our twin sister is no longer physically with us. Here stands blood of our blood and flesh of our flesh, Qi Dom Po. He is a living reminder of the blood oath sworn between Po and Sune Clans, between Black Dragons and Green Mantises."

The elderly woman at the opposite end of the table tapped the floor twice with the staff in her right hand. Her action caused Ma Sune to be quiet.

"Come here my child. Let me get a good look at you." Qi Dom Po looked at Ma Sune, who nodded. He walked hurriedly over to where the woman sat holding her left hand held out.

"Take my hand my child. Let me see you inside."

Qi Dom Po grabbed her left hand. He realized her grip was stronger than what it appeared to be. She felt his nervousness and spoke on it.

"My son, relax. Open your mind. Let me see you." He did as best as he could. She felt the tension fading.

"Good. Good. Now be still, young man." He stood as still as possible. The elderly woman closed her eyes and took a deep breath. Although she didn't open her eyes physically, she opened her spiritual eyes to find herself within his memories. She looked around, searching for the memory that carried the strongest emotion, and found it.

There he was, Qi Dom Po at age ten, sitting in between his father and mother at an international martial arts performance. They were there because of his fourteen-year-old sister, Saki Po was hands down one of the best and she would be performing next. While his mother, Khia Li Sune Po, held her nonchalant composure, he and his father, Han Xi Po, applauded every performer to take the stage. The stage cleared and the announcer came over the loudspeaker.

"Ladies and Gentlemen! Coming to the stage, at the age of fourteen, she has already excelled in twelve styles of martial combat. She's proven to be proficient with thirteen different weapons, and she's the top of her class! Give it up for Beijing's finest young warrior, Saki Po of the Po Clan!"

Everyone from China, except for her mother, stood to their feet, giving her a standing ovation. Looking serious and fierce as ever, Saki bowed in all cardinal directions and began her performance.

She performed ten different katas without a stumble. At the end of the tenth kata she bowed, and those watching whistled and applauded her.

Saki turned to face her mother, father, and brother, and bowed before beginning her next performance. The drummers started drumming. Gracefully, she started the dance of the Dragon. The room was soundless except for the sound of the drums. Her performance was flawless.

As soon as she reached the end of the Dragon, the drummers changed the tempo. She transitioned perfectly into the dance of the Mantis. During the entire performance she never took her eyes off her mother. And when it was over, Saki bowed, and everyone, including Khia Li Sune Po, stood in silence and bowed back. Qi Dom Po and his parents sat and enjoyed the reset of the performances. All of them were very entertaining to Qi Dom Po, but none of them topped his big sister's. In his mind, she could beat them all.

The summit came to an end. Qi Dom Po and his parents met up with Saki on the way out. He high five with his sister and told her she was the best of the best. Everything was going great until they reached the car.

Three men dressed in black business suits approached his father, asking to have a word with him. Qi Dom Po heard Saki's name mentioned in the same sentence with the High Council by the short pudgy man his father called General Chan. Whatever it was, Han Xi Po told him no. And that was his final answer.

General Chan became furious. "Master Han Xi Po, you dare go against the wishes of the High Council? You know the consequences for rebels is death. Just hand over your daughter now and we'll pretend this little misunderstanding didn't happen."

"General Chan Chou, I thought I made myself clear. The answer is no. Go back and tell your masters that Master Han Xi Po said no, and the Po Clan is slave to no one."

The short pudgy general refused to look weak in the presence of the two men with him. "They said you might rebel, so I brought along some who might help you think rationally. Master Li Chang?"

Out of the shadows came the eight assassins dressed in dark brown ninja suits. Qi Dom Po's father didn't give them the opportunity to surround them. He caught the man in the business suit closest to him with the death touch, crushing his windpipe. The general stepped out of the line of attack, but his other cohort suffered the same fate as the first by the hands of Han Xi Po.

Seeing her husband act, Khia positioned Qi and Saki behind her. "General Chan Chou, we don't have to do this. Just walk away."

"You know I can't do that, Master Khia Li Sune Po."

All the ninjas, except for the three who stood long side the general, started circling around Qi Dom Po and his family. Khia and Han didn't wait for them to attack and they beat the assassins to the punch. She struck her first opponent with an open palm buddha palm strike to the solar plexus, which sent him to his death immediately. As he fell, she drew his dagger out of its sheath and threw it, catching the one directly behind her in the throat.

Khia and Han fought to clear a path for Qi and Saki to run to safety. Once cleared, Han told them to run and don't look back. They obeyed. He tried to get his wife to run with their children but she refused.

Standing back to back, they fought and killed several of the ninjas bare handedly. Would've killed them all if it wasn't for the cowardice of the general, who pulled his side arm and shot them down. From that moment forward, the memory became a blur of emotions. The tears that filled Qi Dom Po's vision was unmistakable.

The elderly woman took a deep breath and sighed. She opened her eyes, having seen all she needed to see. "My child, you suffered such great loss at such a young age. We all shared in your loss." She let go of Qi Dom Po's left hand before standing to her feet and addressing the entire clan.

"This sun I've learned the truth behind the deaths of my daughter, Khia Li Sune Po and Han Xi Po. To introduce myself, so that my grandson shall know me by name, I am Elder Mae Za Sune of the Sune Clan. The murderers of our kindred spirits still live. As the blood oath cannot be broken between Sune and Po, we will not live peacefully until the blood of our enemies soaks the sand beneath our feet."

As she spoke, Mae Za Sune rested her right hand on Qi Dom Po's right shoulder and stared into his dark brown eyes. "Qi Dom Po, son of Masters Khia Li Sune Po and Han Xi Po, as the blood oath lives within us all, especially you and your sister, before the new moon, justice shall be served."

Everyone stood to their feet. One at a time, they greeted Qi Dom Po. Once the greeting was over, they went about their personal duties. Ma Sune told Qi Dom Po to accompany her to her study.

They walked from the dining hall in silence because Ma Sune was in deep thought. She'd heard the story of what had taken place the night her sister died, but she'd heard nothing concerning the murder her mother, Mae Za Sune, had revealed. Now, she was curious to know who the enemies were her mother spoke of.

She and her nephew entered her study. She told her nephew to lock the door behind him and have a seat afterwards. He did as he was told and sat in the chair directly in front of Ma Sune's desk. Just as she was about to speak, her phone vibrated in her right pocket. She pulled it out and answered, "Hello?"

"This is General Chan Chou."

"I know who you are. How might I assist you?"

"Master Ma Sune, I was calling to inform you of my team's departure on the evening flight to the United States. After they take care of business there, our clans shall unite and seek them out here and destroy them. The Po Clan shall cease to exist."

Annoyed by the general's ignorance and arrogance, Ma Sune sighed before speaking. "I see you've thought this through."

"Indeed. Listen, I have to make a couple important calls to ensure my team a private flight. I'll contact you if anything comes up where your expertise is required."

Ma Sune didn't bother responding. She simply disconnected the call and placed it on top of the desk. Qi Dom Po sat silently, anticipating questions. And Ma Sune obliged his anticipation.

"Qi Dom Po, do you know who killed your parents?"

"I remember three of their names and the features of one face. The others were ninja."

"What were their names?"

"I recall something about the High Council. Then there was a Master Li Chang and General Chan Chou."

"The General Chan Chou? Short and round about the belly?"

"That fits his description. I could've sworn I heard his voice the night the officers arrested me for no reason and took me to the station's holding facility."

"Do you have a number where we can reach your sister? The same people who killed your parents are out to kill her and her allies."

"Of course, I do, Aunt Ma Sune. I have Saki's personal cellphone number."

Ma Sune pushed the phone across the desk to him. "Call her."

Qi Dom Po picked up the phone and dialed his sister's number. Before it started ringing, he handed Ma Sune the phone.

After the third ring, the line connected, and a feminine voice came on the other end. "Hello?"

"Hi, is this Saki Po speaking?"

The broken English spoken by Ma Sune caused Sia to hesitate.

"No. I mean, this is Master Saki Po's phone, but not speaking. I'm Master Sia Po. May I ask who's calling?"

Not up for the formality, Ma Sune got straight to the point. "Master Sia Po, tell my niece to stop training and come to the phone. Tell her Aunt Ma Sune says it's urgent."

Sia hurried over to Saki and whispered the message in her left ear. Saki frowned, irritated that her training had been interrupted. She told Sia to take her place while she took the call. Saki walked over into a corner to be alone before answering.

"Master Saki Po speaking. How might I help you?"

"Master Saki Po, this is your Aunt Ma Sune. Your mother's, Master Khia Li Sune Po, twin sister. I have your brother, Qi Dom Po, here with me now. General Chan Chou had him arrested but I got him released into my custody as soon as I found out who he was."

“Thank you, Master Ma Sune. How will I ever repay you for saving my brother's life from the murderer of our parents?”

“Nonsense, Master Saki Po. It is I who must repay. Your lives are in danger. The High Council and General Chan Chou are sending Brown Locusts led by the masters of the dark arts, Master Li Chang and Xan Khan.”

“And what is it you are proposing we do, Master Ma Sune?”

“They are leaving out on the evening flight. I will make a private flight arrangement for you all, including your allies, for first light. Don't worry about expenses or packing heavy. I'll see to everything you need once you get here safely.”

“Master Ma Sune, your wishes shall be honored. I shall gather everyone together and let them know we're coming home.”

“Thank you, Master Saki Po.”

“Thanks to you all the same, Master Ma Sune. We'll see you soon.”

The line disconnected. Ma Sune looked at Qi Dom Po, waiting patiently to hear the verdict. “Qi Dom Po, ask someone outside to show you to Yishi Pe Sune. When you find her, ask her politely to come to my study with you.”

“Yes Ma'am.” He jumped to his feet.

“Remember, politely ask her, Qi Dom Po.”

He bowed and exited the study. The first person he came in contact with was a young boy around eleven years old. Instead of playing like the average eleven year old boys he knew, this one wielded a chain-linked bow staff, practicing katas.

“Excuse me, cousin.”

The young boy stopped and bowed before speaking. “Qi Dom Po, my name is Yuri Ba Sune. How might I assist you, cousin?”

Qi bowed back before answering. “Yuri Ba Sune, I must find Yishi Pe Sune immediately.”

The young boy gasped for air. *I obviously said something wrong*, Qi thought.

“Qi Dom Po, whatever you do, don't address Master Yishi so formal. You will find yourself in an impossible match to win.”

“So that's what Master Ma Sune meant by asking politely?”

“More than likely, yes, Qi Dom Po. However, I shall escort you to her so I can return to my training.”

Yuri took the lead as guide and showed Qi where to find Yishi. While they walked, Yuri gave him a tutorial on how to find, and where to find, everyone of importance if needed throughout the day.

They came to a clearing where Yishi sat with her eyes closed, positioned comfortably on her knees, on a mat. Qi Dom Po was about to walk out into the clearing to approach her, but Yuri, quick on his feet, blocked his path.

“What are you doing, Yuri?”

“Saving your life. Pay attention, Qi Dom Po.”

Yuri turned around and sat on the ground, facing Yishi. Qi sat beside him. The silence carried an eerie feeling, almost deadly, and Qi Dom Po suddenly realized why.

From unseen hands, ninja stars flew through the air in Yishi's direction. Without opening her eyes or changing position, she unsheathed the short sword that lay on the mat before her and batted the instruments of death away. The unseen hands kept throwing them, and Yishi continued to wield the blade, sending the stars to the ground about her. Not once did she open her eyes or change her position. Yuri looked on expressionless and Qi was in awe. She reminded him of his sister, Saki.

“Qi, pay attention. Here comes the real excitement.”

Quickly, Yishi sprang to her feet. As another series of razor sharp ninja stars came at her, she whirled about gracefully, like a dancing ballerina, evading and whacking them away. Finally, it donned on Qi Dom Po what she was doing. His sister had performed the dance of the Mantis the night of the summit.

No matter what Yishi did, she continued to land in the same spot. Suddenly, the deadly training came to an end. She returned to the sitting position and sheathed the short sword. Seemingly, in a paralyzed state, she prostrated before her body sat erect, and finally she opened her eyes.

With his eyes focused on Yishi, Qi couldn’t help but notice how much she looked like the other women in the family, especially her mother and sisters. He was overcome with a feeling of nostalgia when he saw the close resemblance to his sister, Saki. Yuri, noticing the mesmerized look in Qi's eyes, stood, bowed, and spoke.

"Master Yishi, Qi Dom Po requests your attention, so I have brought him before you. If I am dismissed, I'll be getting back to my training."

"You are dismissed, Yuri," she said, as she returned a bow to the young boy.

Yuri trotted off, back in the direction in which they'd come. When Yishi turned her attention to Qi Dom Po, he bowed respectfully before stating his reason for being before her.

"Master Yishi, Master Ma Sune has sent me to summon you to join us in her study."

She stood to her feet and walked over to him. "Let me make myself perfectly clear. You are not exempt from any rules on this compound, Qi Dom Po. You are Sune just like you are Po."

"This, I already know, Master Yishi."

"So, you think, cousin. Let's go because you're starting to irritate me."

"But—"

"Silence. Walking doesn't require talking. It requires one to be aware, so be quiet and pay attention. Understood?"

Qi Dom Po nodded, and in silence the two walked the rest of the way to Ma Sune's study

Ma Sune had just finished making arrangements for Saki and the others when her daughter and nephew entered. Both bowed, and remained standing, until she asked them to be seated.

"Yishi, how is your training going?"

"I'm succeeding, Mother. I will continue to get better."

When Yishi answered her question, Ma Sune noticed the change in her nephew's facial expression.

"Qi Dom Po, what do you think about Yishi's skills?"

"Master Yishi's skills remind me of Saki, who I consider the best of the best."

"What an honorable comparison. I recall Yishi and Saki training together when they were young girls. The Fierce Daughters of the Sun and Moon is what we called them. You remember that, Yishi?"

"Mother, how can I forget?"

It was a memory Yishi cherished but didn't want to think about if she wasn't going to see her favorite cousin again. The last time she'd seen Saki had been moments right before the summit.

"What's going on, Mother? I know you didn't have Qi to interrupt my training for this."

"No, Yishi. Your cousin, Saki Po, will be on a flight coming home in the morning. Members of the Po Clan were in America as allies and they will accompany her. Whatever else is to happens will be made known upon their arrival."

"This is surprising news, Mother. Please, give me the honor to be the one to meet them at the airport upon their arrival."

"I was getting to that, daughter. You will take a party with you and welcome them home," Ma Sune told her, as she turned her attention to Qi.

"As for you, Qi Dom Po, go gather the members of the Po Clan who're in hiding and bring them here—there shall be no more hiding for our kindred spirits from this day forth."

Qi stood and bowed before leaving. Yishi looked at her mother with radiant joy in her eyes.

"I understand, Yishi. Our time has come." The two sat in silence until the time came for the afternoon ritual.

***

Although the majority of them had just dozed off to sleep, Saki and Sia awakened everyone. They sat in the basement, groggy from being summoned on such short notice. Saki, felt their disdain and thought it best to speak her peace right away.

"Kindred Spirits, I do apologize for waking you from your rest. However, this meeting is nonnegotiable and you won't be kept long. Master Ma Sune, who is also my Aunt, and the sister of my mother, has informed me that there are assassins of the dark arts heading our way. Master She has asked that we honor her by joining her in

Beijing, China, on Sune Clan's Estate. I have agree, so we're all going to China. Our flight is at first light, so you all should resume to your resting."

The majority of the Po Clan members were happy. Actually everyone, with the exception of Jennifer, welcomed the news Saki had given them.

Jennifer gazed Tabitha directly in the eyes. "Have you ever been to China, Tabby?" she asked, somewhat perturbed.

"No, I haven't, Jenn. Why?"

"Neither have I."

Next, she turned her stare at Malice and Angel. "Have either of you ever been to China?"

They nodded their heads up and down. Jennifer raised her right hand as if she were a student in a classroom.

Angel noticed the gesture and dropped her face into her hands. "Oh, boy," she said aloud, clearly irritated.

Finally, Saki realized Jennifer wanted to say something. She stopped her conversation with Sia and had everyone else quiet down. "Jennifer, is there something you would like to say?"

"I've never been to China before so I think I'll be just fine if I stay here."

"Well, Jennifer, what part of *nonnegotiable* don't you understand? Now, return to your room and get some rest. We'll be leaving out in"—Saki looked at the time on her cell phone. It was eleven thirty five pm— "six hours and twenty-five minutes. I suggest you make every second count Jennifer."

Jennifer parted her lips to respond but Angel gave her a knowing look before the words could escape her mouth.

Tabitha grabbed her by the wrist and whisked her out of the basement. She got Jennifer into their bed and they cuddled until falling asleep.

As Angel and Malice made their way to their room, he teased her about Jennifer's annoying ways. Once inside , she pushed him on the bed and stood at the foot. Allowing her green, silk night gown to slide off her shoulders, she let it fall to the floor.

"Come here," he said. As he summoned her closer, he stared at her beautiful, dark-brown skin.

"Come get me," she whispered, allowing her tone to echo the lust she was feeling.

Malice sprang up off the bed and into her arms. He kissed her soft lips and proceeded to pick her up off her feet. She draped her arms around his neck, returning his kisses with yearning passion. Gently, he lay her on the bed and descended atop her body with kisses and caresses.

Angel moaned under the affectionate touch of his lips and hands. He kissed straight down the middle of her body. When he reached her sex, Malice placed her legs across his shoulders and plunged deep inside her with his tongue. Her body tensed from the sudden feeling, but quickly relaxed.

She moaned and grinded to the tempo of the pleasure being conceived. As orgasm after orgasm coursed through her body, she caressed the back of his head and neck, holding and pulling his face into a stronger embrace with her sex. He licked and sucked on her clitoris hungrily, enjoying the sound of her body's response to his touch. It wasn't long before her body tensed up from an explosive release.

Malice stood up and undressed himself before getting back in bed. He rolled Angel over, positioning her flat on her stomach, and began kissing around the nape of her neck and down the length of her spine. Reaching the perfectly round and soft, plush-mounds of her buttocks, he placed kisses on each mound, as he massaged them with his throbbing-hard erection. Demanding a release of his own, he kissed his way back up her spine.

She moaned and gasped for air as he filled her up, making his entrance from behind. He sighed from the sensational of feel of her sex and the softness of her flesh against his. He grinded slowly, pushing himself as deep as he could go inside of her. Her intoxicating fragrance, along with the release flowing around his sex, demanded him to release as well.

Malice lost control. He went from grinding to long-stroking, hard and fast. The sounds of moans and flesh against flesh slapping, caused him to release hard and fast deep inside her. He remained inside until he felt his release had ran its course.

Once he was completely drained, he rolled over onto his back next to Angel. She turned over and rolled over onto her side and laid her head on his chest. “Malice, have you thought about what we talked about?”

“You know I have, Angel.”

“So?”

“Yes, I am in love with you, Angel, and we're going to get married. Matter of fact, once this war is over, we'll get married while in Beijing, okay?”

When she didn't respond, he realized why. Angel had heard all she needed to hear and she was fast asleep. Satisfied with his own answer, he closed his eyes to rest as well. He knew there would be some long days and nights ahead of them.

CHAPTER THREE

General Chan met Li Chang, Xan Khan, and the others at the airport. He'd managed to provide them with all the legal documents required, and five thousand in U.S dollars. He opened the briefcase where he'd stored the passports, and began passing them out.

"Master Li Chang."

Li Chang was five foot three with a paper-bag brown skin complexion and long, silky black hair. Although she had scars on her face, she was still beautiful. She was dressed in a navy-blue women's pants suit that fit loosely. Without saying a word, she grabbed her passport and visa out of the general's hand and moved to the side.

Chan continued to call names. "Master Xan Khan."

Xan Khan was five foot seven solid. If it wasn't for his facial features, one would easily mistake him for being African rather than Asian. He really didn't like the general because of his dishonorable ways. Xan had wanted to kill him the night the general had shot and killed Khia and Han Po, but Li Chang had talked him out of it. Xan snatched the legal documents out of Chan's hand. He looked the general in the eyes, daring him to say anything, but Chan was smarter enough to know better.

He bowed and continued calling names. "Jun Sau, Sue Mae Jung, Tham Zo Pei." General Chan began to feel nervous under the watchful and malicious eyes of Xan Khan. He closed the briefcase and handed it to Li Chang along with the other briefcase which held the money.

"Master Li Chang, all of their credentials are here. All twenty-two passports and visas."

"What's in the other briefcase?"

"Five thousand in American dollars. Listen, I have to get going. Contact me after you land and get settled."

Li Chang didn't respond. She turned around and spoke in Chinese to her team, telling them to board the plane, before boarding herself. General Chan watched as the airplane rolled down the air strip and took to the air. The further away Xan Khan got, the less pressure Chan Chou felt.

Li Chang and Xan Khan sat directly across from one another. She had noticed the silent war between Xan and Chan and decided to speak on it. "Master Xan Khan, I dislike Chan Chou as well. He is a disgrace to the Brown Locust. Most of all, to ninja as a whole. After we return and collect the payment, feel free to do as you wish with the dishonorable bastard."

"It will be my pleasure, Master Li Chang. Besides, it's time for the Brown Locusts to reunite under one master."

***

Qi Dom Po had gathered the Po Clan together in the back of a fabric store. Everyone circled about him to listen to what he had to say. "Elders, cousins, I've called you together to inform you that, my sister, Master Saki Po, the rest of our kindred spirits, and allies shall be on their way to Beijing. That's only part of the great news I have. The other part is Master Ma Sune, who is the twin sister of my mother, Master Khia Li Sune Po, has asked that we honor her by coming to live in harmony and peace at the Sune's Estate."

One of the elders made her way to the front of the inner circle. She was four feet six, maybe weighed one hundred ten pounds and had long, gray braided hair, and undoubtfully, black. Qi Dom Po bowed to her before speaking. "Grandmother Auset Ni Po, do you wish to speak on the matter?"

She braced the top of the cane and bowed before speaking. "Yes, Qi Dom Po. And yes, we shall honor Master Ma Sune's request. It seems the blood oath hasn't been broken or forgotten."

Auset Ni Po stepped in the center to stand with her grandson before addressing the clan. "Kindred spirits, gather your valuable and prepare to journey to be welcomed by our kindred spirits of the Sune Clan."

There was movement on top of the roof. All of a sudden, the covering of the air duct came crashing to the floor followed by three assassins in the dark brown ninja suits. Before anyone had time to react, a ninja dressed in a forest green suit dropped down from the same duct and stood between the Brown Locusts and Po Clan. The Brown Locust to the far right spoke harshly in Chinese, demanding that the Green Mantis get out of their way.

In a calm voice, the Green Mantis responded in Chinese, telling the Brown Locusts she would be honored to take their lives if they attempted to cross her path. The voice was unmistakable to Qi Dom Po. And when the Brown Locusts didn't adhere to her warning, her movements were a dead giveaway. He was about to go to her side, but she held up her hand, gesturing for him to stay back.

The three Brown Locusts surrounded the Green Mantis. Before they could draw their weapons, the Green Mantis attacked. She did a backward crescent moon kick and caught the one standing in front of her, right beneath the chin. The force was so strong, it snapped his neck backwards, killing him on the spot.

While still in the air, she threw the two ninja stars she'd concealed in the fold of her shirt, hitting both targets in the jugular vein. All three Brown Locusts were dead before the Green Mantis' feet touched the floor again.

The ninja took off her mask and bowed towards the members of the Po Clan. Because they looked so much alike, for a moment, everyone thought she was Saki until she introduced herself. "I am Master Yishi Pe Sune, daughter of Master Ma Sune. Not that I am needed, however, I was sent on behalf of my mother to make sure your journey is made without complications."

Yishi turned her full attention to Qi Dom Po, who could tell by the look in her eyes he was in for a verbal and possible physical lashing.

"Qi Dom Po, you must start paying closer attention to your surroundings. As I was following you, I watched and killed ten of these scouts."

"Being that I was in the open, I didn't think I would be followed. Forgive me, Master Yishi. I will learn to pay more attention to my environment."

"I know you will, Qi Dom Po, even if it means I have to train you myself." Yishi put her mast back on and continued speaking. "Anyway, the path is clear for you all to make a safe journey. A welcoming party will greet you at the high gates."

She bowed before leaping into the air and disappearing back up through the air duct.

The Po Clan traveled to their homes, gathering whatever belongings they felt was needed before starting their journey. It was at least a two and a half mile walk, so they made sure to pack bottles of water and tea.

***

The hour had come for their flight. Saki had everyone on the air strip thirty minutes early. Since it was early in the morning, there wasn't much talking being done. And the little talking being done was mostly from Jennifer, voicing how she didn't want to go. As they boarded the flight, she complained the entire time, and continued complaining after she'd sat down in the seat next to Tabitha.

"Tabby, you could've gone. I would've been right here waiting on you to return."

"Jenn, chill. Think of this as a vacation."

"Tabitha Greene, you do realize we're on our way to Beijing which is in China, right?"

"And?"

"I don't speak Chinese, nor do I understand it when I hear it. Besides, there are way more ninjas in China than Jersey, and that's my biggest issue."

Sitting in the seat behind Jennifer, having to hear her continuously whine, had gotten the best of Angel. Without hesitating or giving it second thought, she touched her forefinger to the pressure point behind Jennifer's left ear and applied pressure. Immediately, Jennifer faded from consciousness. When Tabitha realized Jennifer had gone under, it was a no-brainer that Angel was culprit, so she turned and gave her the thumbs up, thankful for the moments of silence.

Malice shook his head out of pity for Jennifer which prompted a sigh from Angel before she spoke.

"Kenneth Freeman, that's considered the nicer version of me, especially to people who are nerve wrecking. Besides, she could use the rest. Trust me."

"Oh, I trust you, Mrs. Freeman to be. I'm just taking notes on what not to do."

Overhearing their conversation, Tabitha gave her cousin another thumbs up before putting her earbuds in and turning on iTunes. Knowing they had a long flight ahead of them, she closed her eyes and let the music put her to sleep.

Saki and Sia sat together in the front. Saki knew Sia had something on her mind so she decided to question her about it.

"Master Sia, what's bothering you?"

"I wouldn't say *bothering* me, Master Saki. Have you explained to Tabitha the choices that awaits her?"

"No, I haven't. When the time comes, she'll be given her options. Not a moment before."

"Understood."

The silence returned and everyone on the plane was asleep.

***

Hia Xan Tu hung up the phone. The information he'd just received sort of troubled him. The other twelve High Council members, Yin Tzu, Vai Ki Hun, Chang Le, Thom Lo, Chen Sao, Mae Lin, Xul Yung, Hie Lang, Don Klu, Ryu Chung, Bulo Shang, and Wen Chu, sat around the council table waiting to hear what the headmaster had to say.

"High councilmen, some of you are new, so I don't expect you to understand the certain decisions made right away. Especially, the decisions we make concerning history."

Head Master Hia Xan Tu looked at Vai Ki Hun, Ryu Chung, and Thom Lo, the three newest members. All three of them had come from respectable clans. Vai Ki Hun was one of the greatest mercenaries of the Hun Clan. Her petite frame and beauty were known to be deceiving to those who didn't know her.

Ryu Chung was a successful businessman slash mercenary of the Chung Clan. His story amongst those who knew him was he was big on assassinations and hostile takeovers of other's territories. Thom Lo of the Lo Clan was just a heartless killer—something his Clan was always known for. They were the three, the other ten had voted in to have sit at the table. Although Hia addressed the whole clan, his words were mostly for the newcomers.

"I've just been informed that the Po Clan in America is led by a master by the name of Saki Po. Saki Po is the daughter of the belated Masters Khia Li Sune and Han Xi Po."

Ryu raised his right hand, and waited on Hia to acknowledge him, before resting his arm back on the table.

"Yes, Mr. Chung? Is there something you would like to say?"

"Yes, Head Master Hia Xan Tu. From my knowledge, Khia and Han Po were traitors. They breeched the contract and rebelled against the High Council. So, why are we discussing history concerning traitors, if not talking about destroying them?"

Hia looked pass Ryu into the darkness. He searched his mind for a reason that would deter him from doing what he was minutes away from doing. When his thoughts came up empty, he inhaled then exhaled from deep within. Staring into the shadows, he gave a simple nod of the head and like a flash of lightening, the glint of steel appeared just seconds before Ryu's head rolled on to the table. Vai Ki Hun stared into the wide-open eyes of his corpse's head.

Hia spoke. "Now, we will have to vote in a new Council member. But, before we entertain that thought, let me make myself perfectly clear. Disrespect to the great masters who are no longer amongst us in body will not be tolerated. Masters Khia Li Sune Po and Han Xi Po were two of the greatest masters born of China. They would still be with us if a dishonorable coward hadn't shot them."

Vai Ki Hun hesitated, but she raised her hand.

"What is it you wish to ask, Ms. Hun?"

Seeing what happened to Ryu, she chose her words wisely. "Head Master Hia Xan Tu, so really there's no bad blood between this council and the Po Clan?"

"No, there isn't, Ms. Hun. Why awaken a sleeping dragon, when you know it will destroy everything in its path to get to you, and destroy you in the end?"

Vai Ki Hun held her tongue. What Hia said made very good sense. Every clan knew the Po Clan were, hands down, the greatest clan of warriors. Next in line was the Sune Clan. The two clans together could wipe out any clan of their choosing.

Hia took the silence around the table as an indication that no one else had anything to say, so he dismissed them. But, not before telling them the voting process for who would take Ryu's seat would take place the following day.

Once they were gone, three assassins walked out of the shadows, removed the dead body and head off the table, and cleaned up the blood.

***

It was 10:37 pm when Qi Dom Po and the rest of the Po Clan arrived at the Sune's Estate. Sure enough, a welcoming party met them at the high gates and escorted them to the dining hall. The cooks had already set the table with dishes of steamed whiting, brown whole-grain noodles, fig cakes, and hot tea. It was enough food to feed a small village, and the one hundred seventy nine Po Clan members was indeed a small village.

Ma Sune and her daughter entered the dining hall from the kitchen. Everyone stood around taking in casual conversation until Ma Sune asked them to be seated. Quietly, they sat down around the table, and gave her their undivided attention.

"Greetings, kindred spirits. Welcome to our humble home. I'm aware that all of you have met my daughter, Master Yishi Pe Sune.

I am Master Ma Sune, the sister of Masters Khia Li Sune Po and Nya Sune. As many may be aware, we are triplets.

I know you've journeyed from a great distance to honor my wishes, so, please, enjoy your meal. After you've been shown to your resting quarters, you'll be able to freshen up and rest peacefully. Sune and Po traditions are pretty much the same, so I don't have to explain the discipline as it pertains to the morning ritual and meal. Again, enjoy your evening meal."

Ma Sune and Yishi bowed and left the dining hall.

The Po Clan ate their share and called it a night.

Qi Dom Po was having a hard time sleeping so he got up and walked outside, into the coolness of the night. He noticed the light shining through the window of his aunt's study and decided to see if she was inside.

He knocked on the door, and shortly after, he heard his aunt's telling him to enter in Chinese. He walked in and closed the door behind him. Ma Sune took one good look at him and knew something was troubling him.

"Have a seat, young man." He sat in a chair off to the side. "What seems to be troubling you, Qi Dom Po?"

"Anticipation. It's been years since I last saw Saki."

"And it's been even longer for me, Yishi, Nya, and my mother. Qi Dom Po, you're not the only one looking forward to a reunion. All the elders of the Sune and Po Clans are looking forward to seeing one another tomorrow, as it will be the first time in decades."

He lowered his gaze, feeling a bit shameful. "You're right, Aunt Ma Sune. Forgive me for thinking so selfishly.

"It's okay, Qi Dom Po. Besides, my daughter has marked you as her personal project."

"Sounds like my funeral. Especially, after seeing her in action earlier. She and Saki are too much alike."

Ma Sune suppressed the urge to laugh.

"As long as you remember to be polite, and not annoying, you will survive."

"Thanks for the reminder."

She shook her head, feeling pity for him. She knew his attitude alone would be too annoying for Yishi to ignore. In other words, knowing her daughter, he would quickly become her human punching bag. *Thank goodness Saki is on her way,* Ma Sune thought to herself, while opening the book before her.

"Qi Dom Po, allow me to entertain you with a story?"

"I'd be honored, Aunt Ma Sune."

She flipped through the story book until she came to a story about a farmer named Ken Jun Pau. Ma Sune read the story to Qi Dom Po:

"A long time ago, under the Shang rule, there was a farmer named Ken Jun Pau and his wife, Sue Pau, and two young sons, Lu Thom Pau and Judo Pau. He worked hard all year round to gather food to trade, but he was still a poor man. One day Ken said to his wife, 'I'm going down to Hong Kong to barter for food for our family. Measure out what's left of our grain.'

When Sue brought the grain from the storeroom, Ken divided it into two uneven parts. 'Keep these twenty measures to feed you and our children while I'm gone and take these six measures of grain and make bread and beer for my journey,' said Ken Jun Pau.

The farmer loaded his two mules with bundles of rushes, sacks of salt, and natron and silks. When the bread and beer were ready, he said goodbye to his wife and sons and led the mules towards Hong Kong. Some days later, as he was traveling through Peiking, Ken Jun Pau's mules were noticed by an official named Koo Jaul Yung. The official was a greedy and ruthless man, and when he saw the laden mules, he decided to take them from the farmer.

The house of Koo Jaul Yung was close to a narrow path, which had a corn field on one side and a poppy field on the other. The official sent one of his servants to fetch him a sheet, and he spread it across the path with its fringe in the poppy and its hem towards the corn.

As Ken came along the path, Koo Jaul Yung called out, 'Be careful farmer! Don't let your filthy mules tread on the sheet I'm drying!'

'Whatever you say,' answered the farmer cheerfully, as he urged the mules into the field to avoid the sheet.

'You wretched farmer,' shouted Koo Jaul Yung! 'Now you're trampling my poppy!'

'I can't help trampling the poppy with your sheet blocking the path,' replied Ken Jun Pau reasonably. But at that moment, one of the mules started eating the crop.

'Thieving beast! I shall take this mule,' announced the official, 'as payment for my poppy.'

'My mule is worth far more than the amount of damage done to your crop,' protested the farmer!

'We'll see about that!'

'I know this is the district belonging to Lord Shogun. He is an enemy to every criminal, and he won't let me be robbed on his land!'

Koo Jaul Yung was furious with Ken for arguing. 'It's me you must deal with, not Lord Shogun! He beat the farmer with his staff and seized both mules. The poor farmer sat down on the path and wept.

'Stop wailing,' snapped Koo Jaul Yung, 'or I'll send you to the realm of silence!'

For seven days, Ken Jun Pau hung around the house of the official, hoping to persuade him to give back the mules and their loads. When he saw that it was no use, he walked on into the city to look for Lord Shogun. He found Shogun standing on the riverbank with a group of judges, waiting for a barge to take them to the courthouse.

The lord never refused a plea for justice, and he ordered one of his scribes to stay behind and write down the details of the farmer's complaint. As they boarded the barge, the other judge said to Shogun, 'Surely there's no need to punish an official for a few skins, or a trifle of salt. The farmer probably belongs to him and has been caught trying to sell his master's goods.'

Lord Shogun said nothing, but he was very angry with the judges because he knew that Koo Jaul Yung was dishonest. It also saddened him to think how hard it was for a commoner to get a fair hearing.

The very next day, the lord read the details of Ken Jun Pau's case and summoned him before the court. Confident that Shogun was a just man, the farmer knelt down and began to speak, 'O Lord, greatest of the great, when you go down to the Sea of Justice, you shall have fair winds. No storm will strip away your sails and your mast will never snap. Truth will bring you safely to harbor, for you are a father to the orphan, a husband to the widow, a brother to the helpless. You're free of greed, an enemy of lies, and a friend of truth. You're an upholder of justice who hears the voice of the oppressed. Hear my plea, heal my grief, do me justice.'

Lord Shogun, who was used to coaxing a few words out of silent, or stammering commoners, was astonished to hear such an articulate speech. He promised Ken Jun Pau that he would hear the case in full the next day and hurried to the palace. Shogun bowed before the Great Lord Tzu Shang and said in great excitement, 'Great Lord Tzu Shang, lord of the beloved land, I have discovered a farmer who cannot read or write, but who speaks with great eloquence! He's a poor man, and one of my officials has robbed him of his mules and trade goods, so he has come to me asking justice.'

Tzu Shang was intrigued. 'As you value my honor, Shogun, detain this farmer for a few moons. Be silent when he pleads and have someone scribe everything he says. Make sure he has enough to live on and make sure his family is provided for. These farmers only come to Hong Kong to trade when their storerooms are nearly empty. Help them, but in secret.'

Everything was done as Tzu Shang commanded. Shogun saw to it that the towns people offered food to Ken, and messages were sent to the country with orders that the farmer's wife and family were to be cared for. The next time Ken Jun Pau came into court, Shogun frowned and spoke coldly to him, but the farmer was not daunted.

'Great upholder of justice, justice is the rudder of Heaven. You're the rudder of this land, the equal of the Great scribe of Heaven, who keeps the balance and is the most impartial of judges.

If you support the thief, who is there left to punish criminals? The desperate can steal without reproach, but you're great, rich and powerful. Upholder of truth and justice, be generous, be just.'

Shogun listened with secret pleasure to the farmer's speech, and a scribe hidden behind a curtain wrote it all down. When it was over, the lord rose and left the court without a word. And Ken Jun Pau went away dejected.

For five more days, the farmer came to court and pleaded his case, but the lord wouldn't answer him. By the ninth day, Ken Jun Pau was desperate. He knew that the rations he had left for his family would be used up by now, and without him, they might starve. The farmer walked into the court knowing if he couldn't get justice that day, he would have to go home.

For the last time, Ken Jun Pau knelt before the Lord Shogun. 'Great one, do justice for the sake of truth and shun chaos and destruction. When the just man meets his transformation, his name is remembered on Earth and his spirit is blessed in the Realm of the light. It's the law of nature. Speak justice, do justice, for justice is mighty and endures forever.'

The farmer looked up at the lord, but Shogun was silent and gave him no sign. 'A man who once saw has now become blind,' said Ken sadly. 'A man who once heard has now become deaf. For nine days, I've pleaded in vain. Now I shall complain of you to the kindred spirits!' He stood up and strode towards the court doors, but Shogun ordered two guards to bring him back. The farmer was sure he was going to be punished for his bold speech.

'When death comes,' he said sadly, 'it's like a cup of water to a thirsty man.

For the first time, the lord smiled at him. 'Good farmer, don't be afraid. Stand there and listen to your pleas for justice.

Ken Jun Pau was astounded when the scribe came forward and read out the nine speeches from a scroll.

'Come with me now to the palace,' said Shogun.

Ken Jun Pau soon found himself bowing before Tzu Shang. Lord Shogun read the speeches to him and he was delighted that a commoner spoke so well and so bravely. He smiled on Ken Jun Pau and ordered the lord to judge his case.

A terrified Koo Jaul Young was dragged into the throne room and flailed, until he confessed his crimes. Then Shogun ordered that all the official's land and goods be given to Ken Jun Pau. So, the articulate farmer returned to his home a rich man, and justice ruled in China."

Ma Sune closed the book. Qi Dom Po remained silent, in a world of thought. She put the book back on the shelf, where she'd always kept it and sat back down.

"Qi Dom Po, the moral of the story depends upon how it resonates with you. It isn't something you have to share with me or anyone else verbally, however, you will always share your morality with everyone and everything, by, and through, your actions."

Ma Sune looked over at the wall clock. It was minutes pass one a.m. "You should go back to your room and get some rest."

He stood and bowed before saying goodnight and leaving the study.

***

Masters Li Chang and Xan Khan, and the rest of the Brown Locusts had landed in New Jersey and made their way to the slaughterhouse, where the guild was supposed to be. When they entered the building, Li Chang became overwhelmed with disappointment, to say the least. Taken aback by the sight before them, they looked on in bewilderment at the dead corpses of their fallen comrades.

After searching the building thoroughly, they met back up in the front part of the store. Just as they decided to move, a group of young men and women entered, shouldering duffle bags.

Li Chang put on her most deceitful smile, stepped forward, and bowed. The young Caucasian male, who stood out front of the eighteen other people with him, bowed back before speaking.

"Greetings. I'm Michael, and the rest of the brothers and sister with me are trainees. I take it, you are guild masters?"

Li Chang looked on the mixed group with pity. *These fools don't know death has come to greet them,* she thought to herself. Still smiling, she responded.

"Yes, we are, and we've traveled a long way to meet with Master Malice. Do you know where we can find him at this hour?"

"Well, not really. Master Malice and the others left with Master Saki Po. They seemed to have disappeared. Even the Po's restaurant is closed."

Although it wasn't what she wanted to hear, she found the information useful. *At least now we won't have to make a blank trip,* she thought to herself.

"So, you're saying, Master Malice nor Master Saki Po resides in New Jersey at the moment?"

"That's correct. Master Malice didn't say where they were going, but he did leave a message."

"And what was that, Michael?"

"To come over and clean the place up, and they'd be back in three months."

Between playing a role and the information she received, Li Chang felt exhausted. The deceitful smile faded and she replaced it with a cold malicious truth.

"Well, Michael, you've been as useful as you were able to be, but your usefulness bares no fruit. Do you know what happens to useless people, Michael?" Li Chang's tone was nonchalant and stern.

Not knowing how to answer, he kept quiet, which was the most common sign of fear according to Li Chang's philosophy.

"Useless people die." Li Chang gave the order in Chinese for her subordinates to kill the young men and women. Her and Xan Khan took seats, leaning back on the counter and watched as the Brown Locusts slaughtered the group. Xan Khan sighed out of disappointment before speaking his mind.

"Looks like we've been cheated out of a great challenge Master Li Chang."

"Nonsense, Master Xan Khan. General Chan Chou is the one who has been cheated. We are only acting as paid mercenaries. Our job here is done."

The silence returned between the two masters of the dark arts as they continued to watch the others ruthlessly mutilate the ignorant of cause for their deaths.

***

Tabitha awakened and realized she was the only person on the flight up. Everyone else was sound asleep with ear buds in their ears, listening to music on iTunes, MP3 players, and other devices. She poked Jennifer in the side to wake her up. It took a few pokes, but she finally returned to consciousness.

Noticing she was awake, she held a finger to her lips, gesturing Jennifer to stay quiet. Next, she led her to the bathroom. Once inside, she locked the door and turned the sign so the occupied sign would be visible on the outside, just in case someone woke up and needed to use the bathroom.

Jennifer yawned and stretched before speaking. "What's up, Tabby? Why are we locked up in the bathroom?"

"You ask such silly questions sometimes, Jenn."

Tabitha kissed her on the lips simultaneously unbuttoning her blouse and bra. She sat Jennifer up on the counter next to the mirror and kissed her lips hungrily, while rubbing her thumbs across her exposed nipples until they hardened from the sensational feeling. Then she placed kisses on her throat, making her way down to her breasts. She kissed, sucked, and licked on Jennifer's erect nipples and slid her fingers up her skirt and inside of her moist and heated sex.

Jennifer leaned back and relaxed against the wall as Tabitha continued to fill her hunger upon her breasts, and slowly stroked in and out of her with two of her fingers. She opened her legs wider and moved her hips to meet the thrust of Tabitha's fingers, moaning uncontrollably.

As her body trembled from the release, Tabitha pushed Jennifer's skirt up and moved her panties to the side. Face-first, she dove between her thighs, kissing and licking her perfectly-shaved exposed sex.

"Oh, Tabitha . . . Oh, baby, I love the way you make me feel, baby." Jennifer moaned and whimpered, enjoying every second of their love making. As her climax came, she braced herself and rotated her hips forward and upward. Her whole body shook uncontrollably and didn't stop until Tabitha released her from the pleasurable assault she'd inflicted with her lips and tongue.

"How does my wifey feel, now?"

"Tabby, you know how I'm feeling."

"Good. Now get yourself together."

Tabitha left out of the bathroom and walked back to her seat. Ten minutes later, Jennifer returned to her seat beside her. She was about to turn on her iPad and find something to watch on Netflix, but stopped, when she felt as if something had happened that she'd missed. Tabitha noticed her sudden confusion, and questioned her.

"I don't know, Tabby. I remember we were having a talk, but then everything went black."

Tabitha, knowing what had happened, fought back the urge to laugh. "Maybe all the stressing exhausted you, Jenn."

"Probably so. I've been feeling tired on the regular lately. A few pains here and there but nothing serious."

"Well, how're you feeling right now, Jenn?"

"After what you just did to my body, I feel like the most special woman in the world. Drained, but great."

Tabitha laughed. "Get some rest, Jenn. By the time you wake up again, we'll be back on the ground."

Jennifer closed her Netflix account before shutting down her iPad and going back to sleep.

Angel opened her eyes but stayed silent. She'd heard the whole conversation between Tabitha and Jennifer. She waited until Tabitha put her ear buds back in and closed her eyes before she got up and walked to the front to wake Saki from her sleep. Making sure her tone was at a whisper, she told Saki she needed to speak with her privately.

Saki eased out of her seat, not wanting to disturb Sia who was sound asleep. She stood shoulder to shoulder with Angel. "What seems to be the problem, Master Angel?" she whispered.

"It's Jennifer. You know she's sick, don't you?"

Saki sighed. "Of course, Master Angel. But what more can we do besides make her as comfortable as possible until the time comes?"

"So, you're suggesting we not tell her or Tabitha that she's dying?"

"Master Angel, you know just as I do what lies ahead of us. This is not the time for emotions to be hurled about."

Angel knew a lot more, but she wasn't about to speak on it. "Alright, Master Saki, we shall keep this between us."

"Thank you for understanding, Master Angel. How long do you think she has?"

"A full moon cycle and a half. Any moment longer will be full of pain and suffering." Angel looked over at Sia who slept peacefully. "The way I see it, Master Saki, the illusion ends where the true reality begins.

Being of understanding, Saki simply nodded. She sat back in her seat, and Angel returned to hers. One more secret wouldn't be that hard to keep, Angel thought to herself as she looked at Malice's eyelids slowly open. He was beginning to feel the pressure of being under her watchful eye.

"Is everything good, Angel?"

"Yep. I just can't wait 'til we make it to our destination. The things I've been thinking about doing to you, Mr. Freeman."

"Hm. Sounds like I need to get all the rest I can."

"Yeah, you do that, sir."

With a smile on his face, Malice closed his eyes and dozed back off. She followed suit, thinking about all the possibilities to come. The one thing she didn't have to think about was the fact that she'd soon be married to the man she loved.

CHAPTER FOUR

Morning came, and the Sune Compound was in complete silence. Everyone, including the Po Clan members, was in the courtyard, sitting in meditation. After a half hour had gone by, Yishi stood to her feet and faced everyone. Once everyone else was on their feet, she bowed and waited for them to return the bow, before turning around to lead and begin the morning ritual.

She moved with just as much grace as her mother. Through every pose and every transition, she kept her movement in alignment with her heartbeat. From calm to fierce winds, still waters to rising and crashing tides, she transitioned with perfection, and everyone was able to follow her lead. The energy level within the courtyard was exceedingly high.

As she stood up front with everyone's attention focused on her, sweat poured from her pores at a rapid pace as she transitioned through the sun poses. She was drenched in sweat that filled the air about her with the sweet lily scent of the moon, and the energy within, and about her, came to a calm relaxing flow.

Finally, she sat on her knees motionlessly, allowing the flowing energy to run its course. She prostrated and stood back to her feet, faced her kindred spirits, and bowed. They bowed back before leaving the courtyard in silence, headed to go wash up for the morning meal that followed.

After everyone had freshened up and dressed in more fashionable attire, they sat at the dining table. It was easy to tell the difference between the Sune and Po Clan. One of the most distinctive differences was the Po Clan was dark brown, while the Sune Clan was two to three shades lighter—there was also a difference between the two clans' dress code.

Being that the Po Clan were Black Dragons, their attire was mostly black with some form of a dragon stitched on the back or left, or the right shoulder of the shirt. The Sune Clan was known as Green Mantises, which was the reason they always wore green. Unlike the Black Dragons, whether or not the mantis was woven into the clothing depended on status. Ma Sune, her sister Nya, and her daughter Yishi, were the Ma Sune elders and the only ones who wore formal wear.

The cooks and kitchen help rolled the dishes in on carts and worked their way around those sitting at the table. The morning meal consisted of pancakes, salmon patties, steamed seaweed, baked-chopped crab meat, raw maple syrup, and hot tea.

After the morning ritual Yishi had led them through, everyone ate more than their share. The only sounds heard were the clanking of the eating utensils against china plates. Even after everyone had eaten more than enough, there was still enough food to feed a small village.

The cooks and kitchen help cleared the table and carted the leftover food and dishes out of the dining hall.

Ma Sune broke the silence. She addressed everyone. "Greetings, kindred spirits. If you're wondering what will become of the leftovers, know that we never waste food, or anything else for that matter. It is being taken to villages less fortunate than we are. However, I will not keep you all waiting to commune with one another.

I know some of you haven't seen each other since the deaths of our sister and brother, Master Khia Li Sune Po and Han Xi Po, another matter we shall get to after the arrival of our other kindred spirits who shall arrive any moon now. Until they arrive, let's continue to rebuild our union. Our blood oath is a strength that can't be broken."

Ma Sune ended her speech. She and her daughter stood and bowed, and excused themselves to attend to other affairs.

Mae Ze Sune and other elders of the Sune Clan went about embracing the elders of the Po Clan they hadn't seen in decades. Young and old stood around talking, filling in the blanks of time.

***

After the conversation Hie Xan Tu had with his informant concerning Saki Po, he spent more time in his memories than focusing on other matters. Although the High Council was supposed to vote in a new chairholder, he'd postponed the process until another day. Instead, he had summoned General Chan Chou, and it wasn't long before he walked through the door and bowed before the High Council.

"General Chan Chou," Head Master Hia Xan Tu said, "relax."

The general stood straight and relaxed. Hia continued to speak. "Do you know why I have summoned you, General Chan?"

General Chan thought of several possibilities, but none seemed to register reason enough for him to be standing there. With no logical answer, Chan resigned saying, "I don't know Head Master Hia Xan Tu. Why?"

Hia stood to his feet and began walking around the table. After what had happened to Ryu, having him walk past them, made Vai Ki Hun's and Thom Lo's flesh crawl. He came to stand straight in front of General Chan and said, "Your little blood war with the Po Clan is drawing a lot of attention from the wrong angle, and from the wrong people. The High Council operates in the shadows. You no longer have the support of this council on the matter. However, we will not stop you from doing what you think is necessary. Understood?"

General Chan bowed quickly and replied, "Yes, Head Master Hia Xan Tu."

Hia walked back to his chair and sat down. "You're free to go, General Chan Chou."

He bowed again and left out in a hurry. General Chan got in his vehicle and drove off. He opened the glove compartment, pulled out his cellphone, and closed it back. Scrolling through his contacts, he found Ma Sune's name and called her.

"Hello," her usual commanding tone came through the phone.

"Master Ma Sune, it's General Chan Chou. I have some good news," he said with enthusiasm.

"What is it, General Chan," she asked?

"I just left a meeting with the High Council," Chan said. "Hia Xan Tu informed me I was on my own with the Po Clan operation."

Ma Sune sat up straight in the chair within her study. Since Yishi was with her, she put the general on speaker phone before responding. "So, what's the new plan, General Chan?"

He paused for a minute as he contemplated the plan. "Well, Master Ma Sune," he said, confidently, "after Master Li Chang, Master Xan Khan, and the others return, we shall destroy the Po Clan's stronghold four moons from the moon of their return. Then, our clans shall unite and rule Beijing."

Yishi shook her head in disgust. Ma Sune cautioned her to remain silent before she said, "General Chan, be sure to call me on the sun before the moon of their return, so I can have the Green Mantises ready."

"Okay." He responded with more confidence than before since he felt he had Ma Sune's support. "I'll keep you informed, Master Ma Sune."

General Chan hung up the phone and tossed it on the passenger seat. *I'm finally going to have everything I want*, he thought to himself. Ever since the night he'd shot Khia and Han Po, no one who stood on Clan's law of combat, considered him a disgrace. To him, he'd done what any sane person, who knew Khia Li Po and Han Xi Po, would've done.

He had chosen to live rather than die like all others of the Brown Locusts who had challenged the Po Clan skill for skill. Even his father, Master Choo Chou, had fallen by the naked hands of a Po Clan Master Han Tse Po, the father of Han Xi Po. General Chan Chou remembered the scene and everything that had taken place that day. It was the day he'd first crossed paths with Han Xi Po. . .

Chan Chou and his two brothers, Jun Chou and Lune Chou, was walking around school picking on the less fortunate people. Being fourteen, he was the oldest of the three. Chan noticed everyone was giving their undivided attention to a boy who looked to be close to own his age. The boy was painting a portrait of a girl sitting on a large rock, gazing over the water at the sunrise. It infuriated him so much, he bullied his way through the other students with his two brothers right behind him.

Chan and his brothers circled around the boy. "Stop painting and prepare to fight," Chan yelled angrily in Chinese. The young boy paused as if he was considering Chan's demand. However, instead, he smiled and started back on his masterpiece.

Chan wasn't used to being ignored, so he snatched the paintbrush out of his hand and threw it on the ground. "Now I have disrespected you," he yelled in his native tongue. "Now you will accept my challenge, and I shall defeat you and dishonor you!"

"My name is Han Xi Po," the boy said, before bowing to Chan. "I don't wish to fight you because it would be senseless and of no honor to me. "If you don't mind, I would just like to finish my painting."

"This painting," Chan asked. He pointed at the beautiful artwork and punched a hole through its canvas. "Now, I have ruined your work. Accept my challenge," he demanded.

Han Xi Po's smile faded into a serious yet calm expression. He looked at the other two boys who had both begun laughing. Then, he returned his attention to Chan. "Are they your brothers," he asked?

"Yes, they are," Chan replied.

"Good," Han said, "I accept the challenge, but only if it's against the three of you."

Feeling angry and underestimated, Chan attacked Han, but before Chan had even gotten in striking distance, Han had already surprised Jun Chou and Lune Chou with sidekicks to their stomachs, sending them crashing face first in the dirt. He turned around in time to block the wild punches and kicks Chan threw at him. Chan went low for a front leg sweep and found himself losing consciousness from the force of the dragon knee Han had thrust to his chin. As the other two brothers got back on their feet, he showed them the same mercy—which was no mercy at all.

Jun Chou charged Han, and with perfect precision, Han waited for the initial contact before spinning left and delivering a backward dragon's elbow to the back of Jun Chou's neck. He fell to the ground unconscious.

Lune Chou didn't know if he wanted to attack or flea, besides, Han hadn't given him much time to decide. A roundhouse heel kick to the jaw sent Lune Chou to face the same darkness as his brothers.

Bruised and sore, Chan and his brothers went home. When their father, Choo Chou, saw them, he demanded to know who had done this to them. Somewhat embarrassed, Chan told him the partial truth. He told him Han Xi Po was the one who had treated them in such a ruthless manner. Furious, their father told them to come with him.

With their father leading the way, they walked into the Po Clan's territory. Choo Chou demanded to see Han Xi Po and his parents. The young man who had greeted them, led them to a clearing. When Chan and his brothers saw Han Xi Po training, they coward behind their father.

Choo Chou scolded them for the fear they showed before calling out to Han, who was sparring with his father Han Tse Po. Both, father and son, walked over to greet their guests.

Han Xi Po's father bowed and asked, "You're a man who summons the son of a father and not his father? Such a man's intention must be questioned. What is it you want with Han, Xi Po?"

"Look what your son did to my sons," Choo Chou said angrily, while pointing at their faces.

Han Tse Po looked past the bruises and saw the fear and hurt pride. He laughed. "I assure you, if Master Han Xi Po did anything to harm your boys, he had great reason and they asked for what they received. If they would like to challenge my son again, I'm sure we can have that arranged right now."

Choo Chou turned to Chan, Jun, and Lune and said in Chinese, "You will accept this challenge and restore honor to this family. Understood?"

Chan and his brothers understood, but their father could tell they were afraid. He turned back to Han Tse Po and bowed. "My sons will honor the challenge. Which one will Han Xi Po prefer to fight first?"

Han Tse Po rested his left hand on his son's right shoulder and said with confidence, "Master Han Xi Po will take them all on at once. This shall tell the true tale of what happened. Because whatever happened at school, looking at your son's minor bruises, I can tell you, they were shown mercy." Han Tse Po looked down at his son. "But this time, they will receive no mercy."

"Neither will my sons show him any mercy. Challenge accepted," Choo Chou snapped back.

Without having to be told, Han Xi Po walked out into the clearing and stood, waiting on Chan and his brothers. Their father had to force them by threatening to beat them if they didn't meet the challenge. Unlike the first time, Han Xi Po didn't wait for them to attack him. He went at them full force. Chan and his brothers reaction timing wasn't quick enough, although it wouldn't have mattered.

Han Xi Po ran and leapt through the air with a double forward kick that took Jun and Lune out of the equation. His heels landed in their chest, forcing them down to the ground on their backs, crying in pain. Still standing, one foot on each chest, he turned around to look at Chan, who stared into the calm fierceness within his eyes. Not wanting to make his father look on him with shame, Chan charged in swinging.

Han Xi Po blocked and countered every punch and kick he attempted. And Chan felt the difference between Han's mercy and ruthlessness. His mercy was to bruise, his ruthlessness was to draw blood. And that's what he did every time he touched him.

Han Xi Po countered a wild right wide throw out of fear, with a flurry of dragon elbows. He spun around, finishing him off with a reverse dragon elbow, but Chan found the strength to move out of the way. Before Han could redirect his attack, Chan ran, hiding like a coward behind his father, where his other brothers had already hidden. Han Xi Po came walking towards them.

Chan grabbed hold of his father's right arm. He couldn't take any more of the brutality Han was more than likely going to dish out. His father snatched away from his grasp. And, just as Han Xi Po reached them, Choo Chou attacked Han.

The first thrust kick caught Han off guard. But from that moment forward, young Han Xi Po held his own. His father, Han

Tse Po, allowed it to go on until the realization of what was going on dawned on him. Quickly, as Choo Chou tried to hit Han with a locust strike, Han Tse Po pushed his son out of the way, before kicking Choo Chou in the chest, causing him to fall to the ground

"That's enough," Han Tse Po said as calmly as possible. "Cowardice can't be defended. Take your sons and go."

Choo Chou slowly stood back up, holding his chest. "How dare you? I shall show you," he said angrily, and attacked Han Tse Po. Unfortunately for him, he'd made a deadly mistake.

Chan watched his father get humiliated and broken up. Choo Chou swung with his right, but Han Tse Po caught his fist in mid-swing and broke his arm, before hitting him with an open palm strike to the chest, making Choo Chou stumble a few feet backwards. Chan could see the pain in his father's eyes. He wanted to tell his father to let it go, but he knew his father would do no such thing.

Choo Chou went back at Han Tse Po again, but this time with a series of kicks. Han stood in one spot and evaded every kick thrown. His effortless movement was astonishing to Chan, even though it was his father who was being humiliated. Then the worst happened.

Han caught Choo Chou's left leg in the air, and with a swift low kick, broke Choo Chou's right leg. He let his left leg go, and Choo Chou fell to the ground, crying in pain. Han Tse Po walked over to him and his two brothers. "I hope you all have learned your lessons here today. Now, take your father home," he told them in Chinese.

That same night, drunk and feeling shamed, Choo Chou had taken his own life. It was an awful memory that Chan lived with, knowing his lies had led his father to his death. He had hated Han Xi Po and the entire Po Clan ever since.

Snapping out of his memories, General Chan picked up his phone and called Li Chang, who answered immediately.

"Hello?"

"Master Li Chang, this is General Chan Chou," he said in a stern commander's tone. "How is everything fairing?"

"We're about to board our flight back to Beijing," answered Li Chang. She hung up, not caring to tell him it was a blank mission.

***

Ma Sune and everyone else sat about enjoying the evening meal. The dishes were a variety of squid, shark fin soup, chopped up roasted duck mixed with peppers, onion and garlic, and whole-grain long noodles, with homemade lemon tea for the beverage. Everyone dined and enjoyed one another's company.

Just as Ma Sune was about to address Qi Dom Po, one of the Green Mantises entered the dining hall and whispered in her left ear and exited.

Ma Sune stood to her feet and got everyone's attention. When there was complete silence, she spoke. "Elders, brothers, sisters, cousins, our kindred spirits' flight has just landed." She looked at her daughter and nodded. Without a word, Yishi hurried out of the dining hall.

***

Their flight had landed. Saki and Sia walked down the passenger aisle waking everyone from their sleep. Everyone stood and stretched before attempting to walk. Their legs were numb and wobbly from sitting for such a long period of time.

Trent took it upon himself to unlock and open the hatch. The stairs unfolded to the asphalt. He, along with Saki, Sia, Tabitha, Angel, and Malice exited first with their bag of weapons, just in case there was trouble awaiting them. Concluding the coast was clear, Sia yelled in Chinese for everyone else to get off the plane.

Jennifer hadn't understood what was said, but watching everyone else's movement, it was obvious it had something to do with getting off the airplane. She grabbed her bag and got in line. Once everyone was off the plane and had their luggage, the pilot cruised the private plane over into the hanger. Jennifer looked around and didn't any vehicles. "Where are the cars?" she asked. "I know we're not about to walk all the way to wherever we're going."

Saki was about to respond when the headlights of several vehicles could be seen heading in their direction, fast. Sixteen forest-green Hummers pulled up and boxed them in.

"I told you coming to China was a bad idea," Jennifer said, to no one in particular, as she watched the scene unfold.

The outside doors opened on three of the Hummers and four Green Mantises jumped out swiftly and silently and stood watch, looking outward in the four cardinal directions. Parked right in front of Saki, another one exited the driver's side of the vehicle and opened the inside rear door.

When Saki saw Yishi, she had to calm the emotions that were building up fast. Their eyes met, and before they could get control of themselves, they found themselves hugging each other tightly.

"Is it Master Yishi Pe Sune now," Saki asked Yishi?

"Indeed, Master Saki Po," Yishi answered.

"I missed you so much, cousin," Saki told her. She held her at arm's length.

"I've missed you too, cousin," Yishi replied. "Let's get everyone to the compound. Both Sune and Po Clans are waiting on our arrival."

Without another word spoken, they loaded up the Hummers and were on their way. Saki, Sia, Angel, Malice, and Trent rode in the vehicle with Yishi. Yishi had noticed the odd ball in the company and decided now would be a good time to ask Saki about her. "Who is the devil with you," she asked Saki in Chinese.

"A great friend of one of our kindred spirits," Saki answered back in Chinese.

"Be sure to explain to her that she will not be participating in our rituals, and if she'd like, we can have her meals delivered to her living quarters," said Yishi.

"Very well, cousin," replied Saki. "I shall deliver this message upon our arrival."

Saki realized not much had changed about her cousin Yishi Pe Sune. She didn't try to argue a case on Jennifer's behalf because she knew how the Sune Clan felt about people of Jennifer's ethnicity—no different from what the Po clan felt really. Their elders referred to them as devils.

Actually, the Po Clan distrusted them more than any clan did. They were one of the original surviving Clans of the Shang Dynasty. The Sune Clan was the next to the oldest surviving Clan, however, the invasion of the European nations was the reason for their lighter complexion. It was, indeed, a most ruthless and treacherous memory of history which was unforgettable, and to the majority, unforgiveable.

The only reason Saki demanded Jennifer to come in the first place was she was aware of her pre-existing health conditions. She knew Jennifer would've died before Tabitha returned to the United States, *if* Tabitha chose to return.

Saki thought about the decisions Tabitha would have to make once the vehicle came to a complete stop.

"We're here," Yishi said in Chinese, before they got out of the Hummer.

Angel took one good look around and the memories of an unforgotten past flooded her mind. Without even realizing it, she whispered, "Home sweet home," in Chinese.

Since Yishi was standing close to her, she heard her. She looked at Angel closely. Then, it donned on her who she was. Quickly, she pulled Angel to the side.

"Master Shyan Nun Sune," Yishi began in Chinese and bowed, "I almost didn't recognize you. Forgive my absentmindedness."

Angel bowed back and responded in their mutual language, "Master Yishi Pe Sune, you were but a young one when I left. It feels great to be back."

"Indeed," Yishi agreed. "We shall commune later. Right now, let's get everyone settled and freshened up. Master Ma Sune, and everyone else, is waiting on us in the dining hall."

Knowing where to go, Angel and Saki led the way to their sleeping quarters so everyone could get settled and freshen up.

Saki stepped inside of Tabitha and Jennifer's room with them. "How are you fairing, Jennifer," she asked.

"There are ninjas everywhere, and I'm in a country where the language is foreign to me. I'm scared and I feel helpless," Jennifer said.

"If it would make you feel better," Saki said calmly, "you can remain in your room while we're here. Your food and other needs shall be brought to you. Due to your overly emotional character, it would be the wisest choice for you to choose."

"And you're absolutely correct," Jennifer said comically to mask the fear.

Mission accomplished without having to be as blunt as Yishi had put it, Saki thought. She bowed and said, "Then I will see to it that your meals and whatever else you may need is arranged to be brought to you."

"Thanks, Saki," Jennifer replied.

"No problem."

Saki turned her attention to Tabitha. "You, on the other hand, are required to participate in all Clan activities, so get settled, and freshen up, sister. I will be back to get you as soon as I've done likewise."

Tabitha bowed. Saki returned the honorable gesture and walked out, leaving them to get themselves together.

"Tabby, I have a bad feeling about this," Jennifer said.

Tired of hearing Jennifer complain, Tabitha chose not to comment. Instead, she went and took a shower by herself. When she was done, she got out, and dried off. By the time she'd gotten dressed, Saki was returning through the room door.

Good, Tabitha thought. *I don't have to get my ears beat up.* She left without saying a word to Jennifer. Saki noticed her change in mood towards Jennifer.

"Is everything okay, Tabitha," asked Saki?

"We should've left her in Jersey," Tabitha said coldly.

"You're not the only one that feels this way," Saki agreed.

As they walked to the dining hall, Saki gave Tabitha the run down on the culture of the Sune and Po Clans. After the quick crash course of history, she told her the real reason everyone seemed to distrust and dislike Jennifer.

The historical view opened Tabitha's eyes and mind to a new awareness. “You learn something new every day,” she said.

“And we never master anything because of this learning process,” Saki said.

They made it to the dining hall. Everyone was already mingling, enjoying being reunited with family. Saki noticed both of her aunts and her brother. Her cousin Yishi stood near the head of the table. She watched as Angel joined them.

When Ma Sune looked up and saw Saki, she asked that everyone be seated. Around the table the black and forest green blended together. She waited until there was complete silence before she began to speak. “Kindred spirits, we are here as one whole once again. Sune and Po Clan reunited.”

Malice listened and paid attention to his surroundings. He was confused as to why Angel stood at Ma Sune's left shoulder as if on guard duty. But his curiosity came to an end when Ma Sune said, “This moon has brought us more blessings than we could have hoped for. My niece, Master Saki Po, and other kindred spirits and Master Shtan Nun Sune, who we’ve missed dearly. This moon—”

Ma Sune's iPhone rang, stopping her mid-sentence. She looked at the caller ID. “Excuse me. I must take this call,” she told everyone and left out in a hurry.

Malice's eyes focused on Angel. It almost escaped his mind how many unspoken secrets they had between the two of them. Here it was the woman he was about to marry had a whole other identity. But, what could he say? He had killed people who had pledged their loyalty and life to him.

Trent also looked at Angel and everything made sense now. In a low tone, almost a whisper, he leaned over close to Malice’s ear and stated, “Just when you think you know a person.”

Malice nodded, agreeing silently.

Ma Sune walked back inside the dining hall and stood behind her seat next to Angel. “Kindred spirits, this moon is still young. Nonetheless, something of a serious matter has come up which causes for immediate council. Masters and Elders, we must meet now. Everyone else, you may enjoy the rest of this moon."

The elders and masters stood and followed Ma Sune out of the dining hall and into her study. Present, were Masters Ma Sune, Saki, Sia, Malice, Trent, Angel, Nya, and Yishi. Representing the elders were Ma Sune, Nam Wang Po, Shang Sune, and Ty Po. In all, there were twelve present.

"I just received a call from a reliable source," Ma Sune said, addressing everyone at once. "I was informed that those who seek to do you harm in America are on their way back home. They will be landing on tomorrow's moon. Now, the question is, how shall we proceed? Whatever decision is going to be made must be decided by our elders at this very moment."

Ma Za Sune and the other three elders huddled in a circle, deliberating in Chinese. It didn't take long for them to reach a conclusion. Nam Wang Po, being the eldest of the elders who were present stepped forward and bowed.

"We have reached our decision. We call it *Shadow Dragon.* Green Mantis and Black Dragon moving as one, reuniting the true way of Ninja."

There was complete silence in the study as everyone let the reality of what had been said sink in. Trent found himself traveling down memory lane, during a time he would've never imagined being an assassin. A time when his hands were bloodless. . .

His parents were officers in the United States Military. As fate would have it, during the Chinese election year, they were deployed to China as a show of good faith for the presidential candidate they favored. At the time, Trent was only nine years old. And, due to his mother and father's positions, he had seen and visited most of the world.

That year's election turned out to be one of the most violent elections ever. There was constant rioting in the streets, and people favoring oppositional parties were beating and killing one another. Police vehicles and other government properties were sat on fire, vandalized, or bombed.

He would never forget the morning of the official announcement of China's new Prime Minister. The street of the American Embassy was crowded with angry people, young and old, ready to riot if the election wasn't to their favor.

The announcement was made, and the angry mob started rioting. A couple of them broke through the police brigade and headed straight towards the newly appointed Prime Minister.

Trent's parents were on duty. Seeing the angry man running at a full sprint towards the Prime Minister, they blocked his path, not paying attention to the detonator in his left hand until it was too late. He pressed the detonator and seconds later, the air was filled with smoke, fire, and the stench of burnt and charred human flesh. Unfortunately, Trent's mother and father were among the dead.

Not having anyone to turn to, he found himself roaming the streets and dark alley ways of China. He stole and begged, when he had to, in order to stay alive. He did what he had to do until one night, while he was working his way through the back streets, pickpocketing those whom he felt were well off, he was attacked by two street thugs. They had been watching him work and had laid on him to rob him.

As they descended upon him, out of nowhere came help. He watched as the dark clothed masked figure slaughtered the two men with two strokes of his blade. Without saying a word, he reached his hand out to Trent, and Trent took hold of it. Ever since that night, he's never wanted for anything, nor feared anything.

Seeing Trent in deep in thought, Malice gripped his right shoulder firmly. "Snap out of it brother."

Trent sighed, allowing the memory to fade away. Ma Sune had taken center stage again. "With that being final, when you return to your sleeping quarters, everything needed for our mission will be there. After the morning ritual, we shall train, and those of our clans who will join us on the next moon shall train as well. Until then, let's get some rest."

***

Li Chang, Xan Khan, and the other Brown Locusts were on a plane flying back to China. It was a private business flight, so there were businessmen working from their iPads and other tablet-like devices. There was also a group of young, wealthy businessmen having their own little personal party. They had call girls, drugs, and all the above. Seeing this caused her mind to drift back. . .

Li Chang had cried and pleaded, telling her mother about a situation which involved her husband touching them in inappropriate places, but her mother wasn't listening.

One night while her mother was at work, he'd come home drunk. Li Chang had been in her room doing school work, when she heard her youngest sister scream. Quickly, Li Chang had gotten up out of bed, dropping her laptop in the process, and ran down the hallway to her sister's room.

When she opened the door, she became full of rage and hate. Her stepfather was in the process of raping her little sister. She ran back down the hallway to the kitchen and grabbed the biggest and sharpest knife she could get her hands on. She took a deep breath and ran back to her sister's room.

Her stepfather was still wrestling with her sister, as she attempted to fight him off with all she had. Without making a sound, Li Chang crept up behind him and stabbed him in the lower back. As he went down, she continued stabbing him, over and over again, until her little sister put a hand on her shoulder and told her he was dead. Even then, she spat on him.

That very night, she had written a letter to their mother explaining what she'd done and the reason why. She put it in the cuff of her mother's bed covering before she ran away from home. . .

Now, here she was, looking at a group of men who carried the same traits as her stepfather. With a malicious grin on her face, she excused herself to the bathroom.

Once inside, she locked the bathroom door and sat on the floor in full lotus. She closed her eyes and centered herself. In the matter of seconds, she was outside of her physical body. She wielded two short swords before walking straight through the locked bathroom door and into the passenger pod. Without hesitation, she went through the room like the Angel of Death. In astral body, she reached inside the men's souls and cut their spirits from the cord that kept it within the body.

All the call girls continued to prance about in skimpy clothing not knowing that they were entertaining the dead, Li Chang returned to her body and opened her eyes with a satisfying smile upon her face.

She walked back to her seat and sat back down, next to Xan Khan. She found the sight before her kind of comical. The call girls were actually still prancing about, thinking they were on the clock. She sighed, pitying their ignorance and lack of awareness.

"Excuse me," Li Chang said to the ladies in her broken English, "Why are you still dancing? They are no longer conscious. If I were you, I would take whatever I see of value for my time and my mistreatment."

All it took was one call girl to take heed to her words and the rest followed suit. What they weren't aware of was, they were actually robbing the dead.

Xan Khan watched the scene before him in laughter. He was aware of what Master Li Chang had done.

Speaking Chinese, he turned to her and asked, "Master Li Chang," he said, calling her by name, "what will happen when the flight lands and they realize those men are dead?"

Li Chang admitted to herself silently that she hadn't thought about that. She sighed, and in her native tongue, gave the order for the Brown Locusts to kill them all. Without saying it, they went about doing so with pleasure. The horrific screams filled the air until muted by death.

As if it were nothing, she and Xan Khan sat having casual conversation while watching the blood bath that took place before them. "I wonder how General Chan Chou is going to take it when he finds out it was a blank mission," said Li Chang to Xan.

Xan Khan smiled. " Hopefully, the way I want him to, so I can bathe my blades with his blood."

"That's so ruthless of you, Master Xan Khan," she replied, her smile reflecting admiration.

They continued to watch the mutilation before them. After the other passengers were dead, the Brown Locusts collected the spoils. They took watches, rings, bracelets, necklaces, electronic devices, and whatever else they saw that might've had monetary value to it.

CHAPTER FIVE

Morning came, and as Saki had promised, Jennifer received her breakfast in her room. She tried to be pólite and say good morning to the young lady who had delivered the food, however, the young lady didn't respond. She just sat the tray of food on the table and left. Jennifer didn't know what to make of it.

Tabitha came out of the bathroom fully dressed. Jennifer looked up from her meal with a smile on her face. "Good morning, Tabby. How are you feeling this morning?"

Tabitha didn't respond either. She didn't even look in her direction. Jennifer frowned. "Is everyone around here deaf this morning.? Hello? Good morning, Tabitha."

Still no response. Jennifer was getting angrier with every passing second. "I don't know what the problem is, but I don't have to take this shit from you, Tabby."

Nothing still.

Finally, Saki showed up. Tabitha, although she didn't show it, couldn't have been happier to see her. They left the room, leaving Jennifer alone, fuming in her anger.

Saki and Tabitha walked out and into the courtyard, where everyone awaited their arrival. Tabitha took her position behind Sia, who stood on the second row with the rest of the masters. The elders were on the front row.

Once everyone was in place, and standing, Mae Za Sune bowed towards them. When they bowed back, she turned to face east and began the morning ritual.

It was a slow-paced performance. Mae Za Sune took her time transitioning from one pose to another. She led with perfect posture and form and breathed correctly through the process. Her slow movements enhanced the flow of the energy within the courtyard. Everyone perspired, and they could feel the surge of energy that came with each transition.

Mae Za Sune brought the performance to a closing and prostrated, and in turn, everyone followed her lead. With the morning ritual complete, they silently returned to their rooms to freshen up for the morning meal. Tabitha had chosen to accompany Sia to her room, not feeling up to listening to Jennifer's rants about something she didn't understand or was privy to.

Sia, being of understanding, sat out two sets of under garments and clothes. Tabitha held her hand out respectfully, insinuating that Sia go ahead and take her shower first.

With a serious look on her face, Sia stared into Tabitha's eyes as she undressed before her—for the life of her, Tabitha couldn't force herself to look away.

Her bronze petite body and perfectly curved body was flawless. Not even conscious of her own actions, Tabitha relieved her body of her own clothing. Sia walked over to her and wrapped her arms around her, drawing her into an embrace. Tabitha gasped, the air that filled her lungs escaped between the slightly parting of her lips, as the softness of Sia's body against hers removed the tension she'd been feeling for years.

Sia stepped back and grabbed Tabitha by her right hand and led her into the shower. As they stood beneath the running water, their lips quivered in unison, anticipating what was to come. Unable to resist the thought a second longer, Tabitha's lips pressed gently against Sia's. Enjoying the taste, she kissed her with a fierce hunger to have her.

Sia broke away from the kiss and grabbed the sponges. She handed one to Tabitha before reuniting their lips. They kissed and bathed each other, rubbing longer and gentler on the most sensitive places. When they reached their climax, each one of their wells erupted like lava being spit from a volcano. The feel of the warm water intensified the feeling, making it a magical moment.

Angel and Malice were two rooms down from Sia's. They had showered and dressed for the morning meal. Malice had never pictured her wearing Chinese cultural clothing before. But, seeing her in it added another dimension to her beauty.

Angel caught him staring at her. “Is there something bothering you, Mr. Freeman? You look like you're making plans.”

“Are we supposed to be talking right now?” asked Malice.

Angel covered her mouth. Her reaction got a good natured laugh from him. Although there was some questions that he had in mind to ask, he held off out of respect to the rules. Not trying to break the rules any further than they already had, he continued to admire her beauty in silence until it was time for them to appear in the dining hall.

Trent had finished freshening up. He found the forest-green, loose-fitting, silk clothing accommodating. The only thing he felt missing in his life at the moment was a family. He was thirty-six years old with no wife or children.

That will soon change, he thought. He was about to relax in the bed for a while when the door opened, and Yuri stepped in. By the young boy's presence, Trent figured it was time for the morning meal. He followed Yuri out of the room and over to the dining hall, where everyone else were already seated.

The morning meal went as usual—silent until everyone was done eating and the table was cleared. Tabitha and Sia stared into each other's eyes, speaking the verbally unspoken.

Angel, being the most observant, peeped the emotion and nudged Malice in his right side. Seeing and understanding what Angel was getting at, he nodded.

Ma Sune stood to her feet and bowed before addressing everyone at the table. "Greetings, kindred spirits. I shall keep my words short and to the point being that we have a lot to do. This moon shall mark the moment of our reunification. This moon, our blades shall be washed and stained, by, and with, the blood of our enemy. For all who will not partake in this moon's activity, it is our custom that you must fast and meditate. By doing so, you shall be with us in spirit along with our ancestral spirits. The fasting and meditating must continue until we return victorious."

She bowed and sat back in her chair, at the head of the table. At the opposite end of the table, Ma Za Sune stood, leaning on her staff. She bowed and spoke her peace. "As my daughter, Master Ma Sune, has spoken, this moon is the moon of a new beginning. Po and Sune Clan reunited under the blood oath sworn by our ancestors, who are now the ancestral spirits whose strength I bear witness to within us all."

Ma Za Sune paused as she shifted her weight by changing the way she held the staff. "To give and bring understanding of our true history to those of us who know not, all clans, Sune Clan included, are descendants of the Po Clan, the last living, original clan of the Shang Dynasty."

She looked into the eyes of Tabitha, Trent, Angel, and Malice, and continued. "And the Shang are the same as our kindred spirits of Africa. They are one people. We are one people."

Tired of standing, she sat back down and continued to speak. "After this meeting is over, those of us who shall begin the journey of rekindling the flame of our ancestors within our veins, must go into the courtyard and train. We shall remind all clans of the true way of Ninja this moon forth. There will be no more hiding because our enemies shall drown in their own blood."

***

General Chan Chou sat in the planning room which was his favorite place at the station. It looked like a parlor commandeered by a civil war general the night before going into a battle. Golden light illuminated the room from oil lamps, and the men and women, most of who were Brown Locusts under the guise of military officers, stood around the big tables covered with maps and charts, or traced lines with yardsticks and string on the carefully drawn charts on the walls.

He addressed his comrades while he pointed at a specific coordinate on a map. "Here is believed to be the Po Clan's stronghold. As you can see, they have chosen a very good position for a surprise frontal and behind assault."

He pointed at another spot not too far from the first. "This will be our best entrance way. We can cut through Ling Clan territory and blindside them." General Chan moved the yardstick across the map and stopped at a mountain. "Afterwards, we shall meet up with the Sune Clan here, and from there on we shall march forward to a great victory."

He put the yardstick down and sat on the edge of the table. "Four moons from now is when we shall begin. Until then, continue to train hard. You are dismissed."

Everyone bowed to General Chan as they filed out of the room. After they had left him alone, he took his phone out and called Ma Sune.

"Hello," she answered in Chinese.

"Master Ma Sune, this is General Chan Chou."

Annoyed by his formal speech, she sighed. "And how is everything with you, General Chan Chou? Did everything go as planned in America?"

"Yes, it did," he answered.

It was a humorous moment for Ma Sune because he actually thought Li Chang, Xan Khan, and the others had killed her niece. "Well then, I take it that everything is still as planned."

"Indeed, Master Ma Sune. Their flight arrives on this moon," replied General Chan.

"Great. Do keep me informed, General Chan," she commanded and disconnected the lines.

General Chan hung up his phone as well. He stood and looked over the route he'd planned out. To him, it seemed to be the best possible way to get inside Po territory. Satisfied with his strategy, he walked out of the planning room and headed for home.

***

The training was about to begin. Ma Sune, Yishi, Nya, Saki, Sia, Trent, Malice, Angel, Tabitha, Mae Za Sune, Shang Sune, Nam Wang Po, Ty Po, and several other members of the Po and Sune clans stood in the courtyard. Ma Sune demanded everyone to choose their favorite weapon.

Angel and the majority chose the twin short swords. Saki, Sia, Ma Sune, and Yishi choose single long swords. Trent and Malice grabbed double long swords. Tabitha picked up two short handle sickles. And, of course, Mae Za Sune held on to her staff.

Ma Sune stood on the platform where the rituals guide stood leading the morning, noon, and evening rituals. “There are no doubts in our ability to kill. Killing is an easy task for us all because we were born at war. What we must continue to focus on is our ability to evade and shield.”

Speaking in the Chinese dialect, Ma Sune looked towards the rooftops and gave the command for the Green Mantises to attack. Everyone, including Tabitha, knew enough Chinese to know to protect themselves. For a brief moment, there was complete silence, but suddenly, they heard the sound of the ninja stars flying through the air.

Quickly, everyone rolled left or right, evading the deadly assault of the silent instruments of death. The assault ceased long enough for them to get into their defense formation.

Mae Za Sune, Angel, Yishi, and Saki made up the innermost square. In the next square formation surrounding the others, was Nam Wang Po, Sia, Tabitha, Malice, two from the Po Clan, and two of the Sune Clan.

There were four squares. From the innermost square, every other square continued to multiply by two.

The assault of projectiles began again. This time, everyone was better prepared. Tabitha, with the two short handle sickles, swirled them around before her. Not a single star was able to pass through to get to her.

The only sound was the clashing of steel against steel as the warriors batted down the ninja stars that flew in their direction.

Ma Za Sune was in rare form as she twirled and whirled her staff about from left to right and in front of her, catching several of the stars with it. Her movements were just as fluent and fluid as the youngest of the skilled fighters.

Yishi, Nya, Saki, and Angel rotated about Mae Za Sune clockwise, providing a shield. They batted down the silent instruments of death effortlessly. Ma Sune went flipping and flying through the air to join them. After another series of stars had been thrown, the assault ceased.

Not having trained in such a manner proved to be taxing on the lungs for Malice and Trent. Everyone else seemed to be fine and ready for more, and more came.

Ma Sune sheathed her sword before speaking. "Now, let's see how well we can work together without the use of steel." She looked from wall to wall before giving the command for the Green Mantises to attack again.

As the training went on, everyone had proven to be just as proficient in martial hand to hand combat as they were in the use of weapons. Especially, Yishi, Saki, Ma Sune, Angel, Nya, and Sia. Each of them took on two or more opponents at once. Something the rest hadn't quite mastered.

Mae Za Sune had found herself surrounded by three Green Mantises. They circled about her, and just as they were about to attack, Angel flipped over their heads and landed next to Ma Za Sune. She dropped her staff and held out her hands for Angel to grab onto. Once she did, Angel spent around fast, bringing Mae Za Sune off of her feet. Her heels connected with two of the ninjas' jaws, sending them down to the sandy ground of the courtyard. As soon as her feet were back on solid ground, Angel let go of her hands and quickly sent one of the two remaining assassin's down with a spinning back fist.

Before Angel could deal with the last standing opponent, Ma Sune called off the attack. The Green Mantises left just as quickly as they had appeared.

Mae Za Sune bowed to Angel. "Master Shyan Nun Sune, as always, it's a pleasure and an honor to fight by your side."

Angel bowed back. "Likewise."

Ma Sune returned to the platform. "Kindred spirits, this has been a memorable moment. I ask that we all return to our resting quarters and rest for a couple hours. This sun is still young. Let's prepare ourselves for what's to come. You will find that your weapons of choice, as well as your attire, has been delivered to your rooms."

With that being said, everyone went about their way. Sia and Tabitha waited until everyone was out of earshot before they started talking. Tabitha, not knowing what to say, allowed Sia to direct the flow of the conversation.

"Tabitha, do you mind if I walk you to your room," Sia asked?

Tabitha nodded. "I would love for you to, Master Sia."

As they began walking, Sia began speaking. "Tabitha, I'm sorry if you found my actions inappropriate."

"Hold on a minute," said Tabitha and stopped walking. "What happened earlier was the best thing I've ever felt in my life. You freed me from my lusts and showed me love, Master Sia. Now I have to find a way to break the news to Jenn."

Sia took her left hand and embraced it within her own. "I understand, Tabitha. Take the time you need to do so." She pulled Tabitha into a hug and the two woman embraced each other before going their separate ways.

When Tabitha entered her room, the first thing she noticed was the jet black ninja suit and two short handle sickles laid out on the bed. The second thing to catch her attention was, Jennifer walking out of the bathroom naked, toweling her hair dry. She couldn't even look at her the same.

Jennifer looked at her with a smirk on her face. "Are you still deaf and mute, Tabby? Or are you able to talk now? What kind of foolishness are you into now?"

Tabitha shook her head in disbelief. "Obviously the kind you can't understand, Jenn."

Jennifer looked on the bed and saw the suit and weapons. Her eyes widened from fear. "And what's this shit, Tabby? We came all this way to China so you can become a ninja?"

Where is Angel when you need her? Tabitha thought to herself and sighed. "Maybe you should've been allowed to stay in Jersey, Jenn, because you're starting to become very fucking annoying these days."

Jennifer dropped the towel and put her hands on her hips. "I know you didn't, Tabitha Greene. I know you didn't just call me annoying. After all the shit I've been through since being with you, you stand here calling me annoying?"

Reading Jennifer's body language, Tabitha knew exactly what her problem was. She was in a lustful mood. A mood Tabitha wasn't interested in entertaining. But she knew from past experience, she would either have to fulfil her lust or listen to her bitch. *What the hell. . .* she thought as she closed the gap between them.

She pushed Jennifer down on the bed, right next to the ninja suit, before grabbing her by the thighs and pulling her to the edge of the bed. She thrust three fingers inside of her, licking and sucking on her clitoris roughly, causing Jennifer to moan and scream from the pleasure. The oral pleasure she was giving caused Jenn to release uncontrollably. It was as if she couldn't stop the orgasm from claiming her body. Unfortunately, there was no pleasure in it for Tabitha.

Feeling disgusted, after fulfilling Jennifer's lust, Tabitha went to the bathroom to shower. Afterwards, she dressed in her bra and panties before walking back into the bedroom. Fully dressed, Jennifer's face wore a huge smile while she sat watching television. Without saying a word, Tabitha laid across the bed to get some much needed rest.

Angel and Malice had made love while taking a shower together. Now, they lay in each other's arms. She could tell by his facial expression, he was in deep thought. She propped her head up with her left hand and stared at him. "Malice, what's bothering you?"

He looked at her. "Who are you really? I had to fly across the globe with you to find out about Master Shyan Nun Sune?"

Angel sighed before answering. She could see where the conversation was going. "I'm more than sure we all have our secrets, Malice. That was mine. What's yours?"

Malice rolled over onto his back and stared at the ceiling. "I wouldn't consider this to be the best time to discuss such matters. Nonetheless, once we're done tonight, I promise you there will be no more secrets between us."

She leaned over and kissed him softly on the lips. "No secrets, no lies. I'm going to hold you to that, Mr. Freeman."

The smile that surfaced with the taste of Angel's lips faded into a look of pain mixed with seriousness. "I know you are, luv. I just hope you are able to handle and cope with my secrets just as I am yours."

She lay her head on his chest and let sleep claim her body. Noticing that she'd fallen asleep, Malice allowed himself a moment of rest.

***

The High Council was back in session. Head Master Hia Xan Tu had called for the vote on the new council member. The three candidates stood before them. Chung Li, of the Li Clan, was forty-five years in age with light-brown skin and long, flowing black hair. Standing five foot two, he was a mere one hundred ten pounds. She was a merchant who owned an export import shipping company that leased over thirty ships and cargo carriers. She also had a reputation for dealing in the arcane. It was her way of bringing death to any who opposed her in any way.

After her, there was Sun Zo Shoo of the Shoo Clan. He owned every blacksmith shop in Beijing. Sun Zo Shoo was thirty-seven-years old, five foot five, and one hundred forty-five pounds. Shoo was most known for being a ruthless employer. Before any shipment of blades were packaged and shipped, he would use one of the swords against workers who were reported as slackers on the job. Sun Zo Choo saw this as a good way of testing the stability of the blades.

Then there was Zhia Mi Yang of the Yang Clan. Younger than the rest, she was just twenty-one years in age, four foot eleven, and one hundred fifteen pounds. Her skin was golden like it had been kissed by the sun, and she wore her long jet black hair braided. Zhia was a very wealthy business woman, and a heartless one at that. She was well known in the martial world because of the tournaments she'd fought and performed katas in.

One of the three would soon be chosen as a member. The voting system was simple. Each candidate's name was called by Hia, and the existing board members raised their hand in favor of the candidate they wanted to vote for. Zhia Mi Yang won by a landslide.

With the voting done, the other two candidates were dismissed and Zhia was told to take her seat at the table. Hia stared at her with an emotionless gaze. “Master Zhia Mi Yang, welcome to the High Council. Introductions are not something the council wastes energy on. We think it's best that you keep to your own ideas rather than being influenced by others.”

Having said that, Hia stood and walked around the table. “I sense the rise of the Black Dragon coming. And, I do mean soon. The council will have to make a decision that will either save the lives of our loved ones, including our own, or we all shall fall under the ruthlessness of the Black Dragon due to the ways of our ignorance. I will speak no more of this until the time comes. You are dismissed.”

Everyone stood, bowed, and left quietly. Hia Xi Tu sat in his chair at the head of the table in deep thought. He knew it would be senseless and suicidal to fight against the Po Clan— that, he was sure of. A trip down a memory lane reminded him of his first encounter with the Po Clan. . .

There he was, young Hia Xan Tu, the only child of his mother, Lin Tu, and father, Pan Tzu Tu. His father wanted him to be a great warrior and a successful business man. He wanted the best of all worlds for him.

One day, while he waited for his father to pick him up from school earlier than usual, he watched as one young boy put three other boys to shame. When his father arrived and learned what the three boys had done to the boy’s painting, he told the teacher to provide the young boy with another canvas and that he would pay for it.

Hia approached his father and bowed.

His father bowed back. “My son, who is the young boy who fought the other three boys?”

Hia looked in the direction his father pointed in. “Father, he is Han Xi Po from the Po Clan.”

His father nodded. “I think I should have a quick word with the young warrior. Come.”

Hia and his father walked down onto the schoolyard, where Han sat frowning, upset that his painting had been ruined. Before they could reach him, the teacher hurried over to Hia's father and bowed, handing him the new canvas.

“Han Xi Po,” Hia's father called out, “be not discouraged. Look, I have a new canvas. Han bowed and thanked him. Hia's father looked him in the eyes and replied, “You're welcome great young warrior. I would like to employ you to teach my son, Hia, to be a mighty warrior like yourself.”

Han eyed Hia for a moment, before looking back into the eyes of Pan Tzu Tu. “As you wish, sir. I shall come by every day after school to train with him.”

Hia's father bowed quickly, expressing his happiness. “Thank you, Han Xi Po. Your rewards shall be great.”

Just as Han Xi Po had said, he accompanied Hia home every day after school. Just to be on the safe side, Han's father demanded that two of his cousins go along with him. They trained until Hia was exhausted and didn't feel like tumbling to the ground anymore for the day. When he demanded that he stay for dinner, he realized his father was growing fond of Han Xi Po.

Han and his two cousins had honored his father by having dinner with them. The entire time they sat at the table waiting for the meal to be served, Pan spoke and laughed with Han. Hia became angry with feelings of neglect. He was so angry, he told himself he was going to kill Han Xi Po during the next training session.

After Han and his cousins left, he went straight to bed.

The next day had come and the training was under way. As usual, Hia's father and Han's two cousins sat on the side watching while drinking tea. Hia went at Han with everything he had in him, only to find himself face-first in the grass.

Han noticed he was fighting out of anger and shook his head. “Hia, get control of yourself. You are fighting as if I am your enemy, when I am only here to assist with your training.”

Hia jumped back to his feet and rushed at him again. He threw a series of sidekicks which Han evaded, effortlessly, before sweeping Hia off his feet. Realizing he was no match for the skilled young boy, he jumped up and ran over to the weapons rack and grabbed a sword.

When his realized what was happening, he quickly sat his cup of tea down and stood up. “Hia Xan Tu, what are you doing?” he shouted out, “Stop this nonsense immediately!”

With hatred in his eyes and a twisted frown on his face, he paused and looked at his father momentarily. Then, without a second thought, Hia ran at Han full force. Pan jumped up to stop him, but Han's cousins blocked his path, assuring him it was impossible for Hia to do the young Master Han any harm. Pan sat back down, feeling shame and dishonor.

Hia swung violently at Han with the sword. Han turned a series of backwards flips to put some distance between them before raising his hand. “Hia Xan Tu, you are mad. I ask that you stop before you force me to hurt you. This is my first and only warning to you.”

“Han Xi Po, you shall die!” Hia yelled, and charged him a second time.

Fearless, Han sighed and stood motionless waiting on the attack.

Hia swung and swung, and without moving from where he stood, evaded, blocked, and countered. He'd hit Hia so fast, and so many times, Pan nor his cousins were able to follow. Finally, when he tried to thrust him through with the blade, Han sidestepped and struck him with a dragon fist strike to the jaw, causing him to drop the sword. Dazed, Hia swung and hit Han unconscious with a dragon elbow uppercut to the chin.

Han walked out of the clearing to stand before Pan. He bowed. “Good, sir. Master Pan Tzu Tu, I will no longer be able to train with your son.”

From that moment forth, his father had vowed to never speak to him again. A vow he had taken to his grave. The memory was a painful one because both great masters, Han Xi Po and Khia Li Sune Po's lives had ended dishonorable. He already knew what his vote would be when the time came, and he also knew what would become of those of the High Council who chose to vote otherwise.

CHAPTER SIX

The flight had landed. Li Chang, Xan Khan, and the other Brown Locusts waited to get off the plane. Although the stench of death didn't bother them, they didn't care to remain in the midst of their victims any longer than they had to. Li Chang had suggested they carry their weapons openly since they were back in their country.

"More of a reason for us not to, Master Li Chang," said Xan Khan, in reference to her wanting to have her swords ready at hand.

She simply nodded since she didn't feel the need to debate.

The aircraft came to a complete stop. Li Chang ordered one of the Brown Locusts to knock on the door of the cockpit where the pilot was. Already knowing the co-pilot would be the one to answer and open the door, Chang gave the order to kill both, the pilot and co-pilot.

No questions asked, the Brown Locust did as she was told and executed both. Without a second thought, she returned to the interior of the plane just as quickly as she'd left.

Xan Khan opened the passenger door of the plane and enjoyed the fresh air that filled his lungs. With their baggage slung across their shoulders, they made their exit. They were so glad to be home, neither of them paid attention to their surroundings.

The ninjas dressed in forest green and jet black lined the top of the aircraft, waiting on the perfect time to descend.

Eight of the assassins who were on top of the plane held portions of a net—the other four had their weapons drawn. Ready to spill blood, they waited for the signal to be given. They watched as the Brown Locusts walked out into the open and found themselves surrounded by eight Black Dragons, and eight Green Mantises, with swords and sickles already drawn. Just as Li Chang and the others dropped their bags, one of the Green Mantises on top of the airplane gave the signal.

Before the Brown Locusts could get into their defense stance, the net descended upon them. The eight continued to hold the net, trapping their enemies inside. The other four assassins joined the sixteen who surrounded the Brown Locusts as they tried to flee, but to no avail. The twenty ninjas thrust the blades of their swords and sickles through the net, piercing their enemies' flesh.

Their blood ran thick over the smoothly paved airstrip. The assassins didn't stop thrusting their blades in them until there was no more movement beneath the net. The signal was given for the eight to remove the net. Once the net was removed, they carried it with them as they disappeared into the shadows.

In a rapid pace, the Black Dragon with the short-handle sickles went about severing the heads from the bodies of the dead corpses. Once done, the rest of the assassins disappeared in the shadows.

***

Qi Dom Po and all the other members of the Sune and Po Clans remained in the courtyard, in meditation and fasting. Every so often, they would transition out of full lotus to sitting erect on their knees, before prostrating. They had been doing this since the moon appeared in the heavens. And, here it was approaching midnight.

As they prepared to transition back to full lotus, it was like a whisper on the winds when they returned from the slaughter of their enemies. All twenty eight of the ninjas bowed and disappeared again.

Instead of transitioning back to full lotus, Qi Dom Po and the other prostrated, giving praise knowing they had been victorious and not one of their kindred spirits had fallen by the blades of their enemies. They stood to their feet and left the courtyard, heading to their sleeping quarters in high spirits.

***

Angel and Malice returned to their room and showered. They lay in the bed in casual conversation until Angel brought up the conversation from earlier. "Alright, Kenneth Freeman aka Master Malice, it's time to put all of our secrets behind us. What demon haunts you the most?"

Malice sighed, knowing what he was about to reveal wouldn't be taken lightly. "I was the one who killed John in the alley that night. He was out to kill Tabitha."

She looked at him surprisingly. "Damnit, man. But I guess I can see how that happened. Is that it?" she asked, with her head tilted to one side.

Malice swallowed hard. "Nope. I killed Mickey because he was the one who put the contract out on Tabitha."

Angel's mouth opened wide. "I—" Then it dawned on her. Valencia's body had been found inside of Mickey's attic right next to him. It was either a coincidence, or what happened was something Angel didn't care to, or *want* to believe. "Malice, you do know that Valencia's body was found next to Mickey's, don't you?"

He nodded. "Yes, Angel, I know. I tried to talk her out of pursuing Tabitha. I had watched them fight at the substation. It was actually a damn good fight until Valencia switched gears. That's when I intervened. Had I not, Tabitha would've died."

Angel's nose flared, her eyes widened, and the tone of her voice went up an octave. "Fuck the reason why, Malice. Did you kill Valencia, too?"

The painful look on his face, along with the tears that filled his eyes, told her what his words couldn't.

"Malice, how could you? Valencia was a true sister to the guild, and the closest thing I had to a real sister."

"She forced my hand, Angel," he said, "and If I could go back and do things differently, I would," he added.

"But you can't, Malice. Goodnight." She turned over on her side so that her back was toward him.

He tried to comfort her, but she snatched away. "Don't fucking touch me."

Malice rolled over and got out of bed. He made him a pallet on the floor and went to sleep.

***

Tabitha wasn't sleepy at all. She sat on the floor in her room cleaning her weapons. Her thoughts were really on Sia, wondering if she was still awake and doing the same thing.

Jennifer sat up in the bed and watched her. “Tabby, this is too much for me,” she admitted. She shook her head from side to side slowly.

Tabitha continued to remove the bloodstains from the short handle sickles. “What's the problem now, Jenn?”

Jennifer laughed. She couldn’t believe how blind Tabitha was to her feelings. “You’ve become a ruthless killer, Tabitha. You all are no better than the people you've slaughtered.”

Her last comment really got under Tabitha's skin. “So says the person who works for the federal government.” She paused, turned her gaze toward her, and rolled her eyes. “Jenn, before you say some shit you won't be able to take back, I advise you to let whatever you're thinking go.” Now, she was the one shaking her head from side to side. She rolled her eyes again and returned her focus back in the direction of her weapon.

Jennifer slid to the edge of the bed. “Maybe it's time for us to call it quits. My life has been a living hell ever since I met you and your people.”

And that was what Tabitha tried to prevent. She put down the cloth and sickle and stood to her feet. “I promise you; your ass will be on the first thing flying, sailing, or smoking once this is over. I'm glad you decided to show me your true colors.” And with that said, Tabitha stormed out into the bathroom to shower. After she finished, she got dressed and stormed out of the room without saying another word.

She found herself standing in front of Sia's room door. As she lifted her hand, preparing to knock, the door slid open and Sia grabbed her by the wrists and pulled her inside. After closing the door and locking it, they lay in the bed cuddling until they fell asleep.

***

Hia and his wife Shai were sound asleep when his phone rang. He thought he was dreaming, until he opened his eyes and noticed the bright florescent color of his phone's screen lighting up. His mouth opened wide, forming a disfigured O-shape as he yawned and stretched. Wiping the cold from his eyes, he reached over and got his phone. "Hello?" he answered in a raspy voice.

"Head Master Hia Xan Tu," the female caller said, "this is Master Zhia Mi Yang speaking. I'm sorry for disturbing you at such an hour, however, I figured you would want to receive this information before the authorities."

Hia looked at the time on his phone. It was 2:25 am. He got up out of the bed and took the call to another room, not wanting to disturb his wife's rest. "Master Zhia Mi Yang, you have my undivided attention. What's the problem?"

Zhia scrolled her text messages until she found the text she was looking for. She opened it. "Master Li Chang and Xan Khan, and their company are all dead. Correction. They were slaughtered and beheaded on the airstrip after their flight landed."

Now Hia was wide awake. "Any idea who could've done this, Master Zhia?"

She read further into the message. "Yes, Sir. My scout's report reads: Black Dragons and Green Mantises."

Hia sighed. "So, it has begun. Thank you, Master Zhia. Be in no doubt that you are not to speak to anyone else concerning this matter."

Hearing the sternness of Hia's tone, she deleted the text immediately. "Text expunged, sir." She hung up.

Hia Xan Tu pressed the phone receiver icon ensuring the call had disconnected. With the Po and Sune Clans united again, it would be foolish not to propose a treaty. *And just when I thought it couldn't get any worse.*

With that thought in mind, he walked back into the bedroom and got back in bed. He pulled his wife close and held her tightly until he fell asleep.

***

Morning came quickly, and Ma Sune was on her way to the courtyard for the morning ritual. She let everyone, who partook in the previous night's mission, know that they didn't have to partake this morning. But when she entered the courtyard, there they were, ready to begin. And Saki was already standing on the platform facing them.

Once Ma Sune took her place within the ranks, Saki bowed, faced east, and began the ritual. Her movement and form was dance-like. She flowed through every emotional state, of each element, effortlessly. As Qi Dom Po watched her, he couldn't help but feel nostalgic because it was like watching her performance at the summit all over again.

At the end of the ritual, Saki prostrated and remained sitting on her knees. Although her words were meant for everyone in attendance, she stared into Tabitha's eyes as she spoke. "I know it is Sune Custom to remain silent until after the morning meal, however, kindred spirits, at this moment, one of our sisters shall make the decision to rebirth the Black Dragon spirit within her."

They bowed. Saki returned the honorable gesture before looking back at Tabitha. "Sister Tabitha Greene, come forth."

Saki was still sitting on her knees, and without hesitating, Tabitha hurried up to the platform and stood next her. She bowed, and Saki bowed back and continued to speak. "Sister Tabitha Greene, you have fought by our side as a Po. Do you accept this offer?"

Tabitha looked toward Sia and nodded. "Yes, Master Saki Po, I accept."

Saki stood to her feet and faced Tabitha. "Are you prepared to embrace the Black Dragon spirit within you?"

"Yes, Master Saki Po, I am prepared," answered Tabitha with a serious expression.

Saki bowed and walked off to stand next to Sia and Yishi. "As a Black Dragon, you are your most superior weapon."

Saki turned to her cousin Yishi and nodded.

In a calm tone, Yishi, commanded the Green Mantises to attack, and down came a series of ninja stars from unseen hands. Tabitha dove through the air. She tucked and rolled onto the sand, evading the first oncoming assault.

The silent instruments of death continued toward her and she continued evading them. She twisted through the air, back dropped, and rolled around left and right in the sand. Finally, the razor-sharp projectiles ceased from flying. Then, four Green Mantises seemed to step out of the walls before surrounding her.

They unsheathed their blades and moved in to attack. Tabitha barely escaped the first assault. They went for a thrust strike inches away from her head but she went down into a full split. Using her speed and agility, she went into a cyclone leg sweep, catching the four attackers off guard.

As they tumbled to the ground Tabitha rolled over, on top of the one closest to her, and delivered a series of elbows until he bowed out of the fight. Before she could get to another one, the other three were back on their feet and they had changed their attack formation. Instead of all three coming at her at one time, two attacked while the other stood a few feet away.

Tabitha sidestepped the sword attack that came from her left. Before she could counter, she found herself having to weave a slashing attack that came from the right. As she stood erect, the third assassin threw a ninja star, causing her to back drop. She sprang back to her feet and quickly struck the one on her right with a side kick to the solar plexus, sending him crashing to the ground. Before she could get to the last two, Yishi called off the attack.

Respectfully, the four Green Mantises and Tabitha bowed to one another. She watched as they scaled the side of the buildings and disappeared from sight. She was definitely winded. However, she wasn't tired which was a good thing.

Saki gave Tabitha a minute to catch her breath. When she saw her breathing had become calm, she looked at Sia and nodded. Sia bowed. She performed a series of flips and stood directly in front of Tabitha. She bowed, and likewise, Tabitha did the same.

Angel and Malice stood side by side watching the initiation process. They hadn't said anything to one another since the previous night. Feeling guilty, he sighed and broke the silence. “Angel, I—”

“Malice, I love you. The past is the past. Just don't ever do anything so stupid again.”

The pressure he'd been feeling dissolved. “I promise you, I won't.” He looked toward Tabitha and Sia. “Who do you like in this match?” he asked Angel, as they waited for the two to compete in martial combat.

Angel smirked. “Your cousin is a mean fighter, but Sia is about to give new meaning to the phrase *beat-down*.”

Not doubting her word, he nodded. “So, how does this phase of the initiation work?”

Angel watched as they stood toe to toe in their defense stances. “It will go on until Tabitha strikes Sia.”

Malice frowned. “How hard can that be? Tab is gonna get through this with no problem.”

Angel shook her head. “I doubt it. Let me explain it to you in the terminology that best fits what's about to happen: your cousin is about to get her ass handed to her.”

Both, Tabitha and Sia’s facial expression was stern and emotionless. They stared at one another intently, without blinking an eye.

Finally, Tabitha attempted to strike Sia, but she couldn't. Each time she found herself being a victim to counter attacks—so fast, it was nearly impossible to see them coming. She threw a series of kicks before trying to surprise Sia with a spinning back fist. Reacting with swiftness, Sia caught, and delivered, multiple open palm strikes to Tabitha's body, before taking her down with a chip toss.

Slow at getting back to her feet, Tabitha decided to change up her offense. She came at Sia with a flurry of elbows. Sia stood still and blocked elbow after elbow, and in between blocks, she struck Tabitha with closed fists to the face, drawing blood.

Tabitha, realized she had Sia focused on blocking and countering her flurry of elbows, went for what she knew. As Sia went for a strike to her jaw, she spent and struck her with a ridge hand to the back of the neck.

As Sia stumbled forward, Tabitha took her on to the ground with a scissor leg take down. She rolled over on top of Sia, and in a sitting position held her arms down. She stared in her eyes, breathing hard and bleeding from her nose and lip.

"Halt," Saki yelled. "Sister Tabitha Greene, you have proven yourself worthy to the Black Dragon spirit within."

Tabitha stood to her feet and pulled Sia up with her. They faced each other and bowed. Saki, Yishi, Ma Sune, Nya, Angel, Trent, Malice, Ma Za Sune, Nam Wang Po, Shang Sune, and Ty Po joined them on the platform. Everyone bowed to each other.

Saki nodded approvingly to Tabitha. "And now the Elders shall reveal the name of the Black Dragon Spirit within Sister Tabitha Greene.

Mae, Ty, Nam, and Shang stood off a bit from the others in communion. Ten minutes later, they walked back over to join the masters and Tabitha.

Nam Wang Po greeted Tabitha with a bow. "You shall no longer be called or known as Tabitha Greene. It would be a great disrespect to the Black Dragon Spirit within. From this sun forth you are Moon Tao Po, The way of the Illuminated Black Dragon."

Everyone chanted, "Moon Tao Po!" over and over again until Ma Sune raised her hands, beckoning them to be silent.

"This has been a great start of the sun. Now, let's return to our quarters and freshen up for the morning meal."

The clans dispersed. Everybody had left Sia and Moon standing on the platform. Sia looked at her bloody and bruised face with concern. "Are you okay, Moon Tao Po? Would you like for me to escort you to your room?"

She shook her head. "Thank you, Master Sia, but I'm good. Just a reminder of why I shall never make you mad."

Sia smirked. "Moon Tao Po, not trying to sound offensive, but that was me taking it light on you. Nobody has ever seen me mad. I don't think *I* ever want to see me mad."

Moon laughed. "If that's you at sport, you're absolutely right. I'll see you at the morning meal, Master Sia. Then, if you wish, I will see you tonight."

The two women embraced and went their separate ways. Moon Tao Po made it to her room. Inside, she closed the door and allowed her body to collapse on the floor. Jennifer's eyes were glued to the TV screen until she heard the loud *thud!* Of her body hitting the floor.

Jennifer got up off the bed and rushed over to her side. "Tabby, what in the hell happened to you? Tabby!"

Not knowing what to do, Jennifer ran to the door and opened it to find Angel standing with her hand up ready to knock. She frowned at the hysterical look on Jennifer's face. "What's wrong with you, Jennifer?"

She walked in, closed the door, and locked it behind her. "You allowed this to happen to Tabby," Jennifer said accusingly.

Angel shook her head out of pity. "Jennifer, for the first and final time, sit down and shut up before I shut you up. Understood?"

Jennifer wasn't hearing any of that. "How can you be so calm and cool about this, Angel? None of you are really her friends. I knew all of you were bad for her. I knew it."

Angel sighed, as her annoyance began to surface. "First of all, my name is Shyan Nun Sune and hers is Moon Tao Po. And secondly, you're right, she's not my friend, she's my sister."

With that being said, Shyan struck Jennifer behind her right ear with a pressure point strike, with lightning-fast movement. As her body fell limp and unconscious, Shyan dragged her over to the bed and returned to Moon's side. "Moon Tao Po, can you hear me?"

She nodded and replied, "Of course I can. I'm beat up, not deaf or dead."

"Good," replied Shyan, "because I need you to listen very carefully so we can have your body healed. Are you ready?"

Moon nodded again. "I'm listening. Let's do it, Master Shyan."

Shyan Nun Sune lay down next to Moon Tao Po. "This craft isn't much different from the other. Only this time, you must totally focus on traveling within your body. The surface is only a reflection of the inside. Are you following me?"

Moon nodded and closed her eyes. When Shyan noticed she'd begun concentrating, she continued. "You must travel to the injured portions of the body. Flow to each injury and touch it, willing it to be healed."

Moon Tao Po followed Shyan's instructions to the tee. She began to see the inside of her body. Shyan continued to guide her through the process. "Moon Tao Po, you're doing great. Now, travel to the parts that are inflamed. It is there you must touch with your will with the intent to heal the body. You will know if you have successfully done so because the red will fade into an emerald green color."

Moon was able to see exactly what Shyan was speaking of. She touched the inflamed parts within, and the pain receded as the green light spread throughout the muscles, joints, and nerves.

On the outside, Shyan watched as the visible bruises and swelling disappeared, as if its initial being was only an illusion. With all visible marks of battle gone, she guided Moon back out of the in-depth art.

Moon Tao Po's eyelids shot open wide. "Wow!"

Shyan helped her to her feet. She wobbled a little, so she kept a hand on her shoulder.

"Easy there, youngster. You might be healed, but it still takes a minute to get oriented after doing such things. How are you feeling?"

Moon stretched and yawned. "I feel like a newborn baby." She bowed. "I can never thank you enough, Master Shyan Nun Sune."

Shyan bowed back. "Oh, but you can, Moon Tao Po." Shyan looked over at Jennifer's unconscious body lying on the bed. "When this is all over, get rid of that bitch."

Moon nodded. "I plan on it. You have my word, Master Shyan Nun Sune."

Shyan looked over at Jennifer's body again and shook her head out of disgust and pity. "Let me leave you to get yourself cleaned up. I'll see you at the morning meal." She made her exit and closed the door behind her.

Moon got her shower out of the way and got dressed. She looked in the mirror, admiring the jet-black silk linen with the dragon on the back of the shirt. She didn't even glance Jennifer's way when she left the room. She quickly made her way to the dining hall, where everyone were seated awaiting her arrival.

Moon bowed as she entered the room before taking her seat across the table from Sia. The meal was then carted out and the cooks and kitchen help set the table. Afterwards, they left to wash their hands, and moments later, returned to their seats at the table. After they returned, the eating began.

No one spoke a word while eating. Ma Sune was enjoying her plate of baked Salmon and biscuits with apple jelly when her cellphone rang.

She looked at the caller ID and stepped away from the table before answering. "General Chan Chou, you have a knack for calling at the wrong time. I'm trying to enjoy my morning meal. What is it?"

The general looked at the scene before him. "I apologize, Master Ma Sune. Regrettably, I have disturbing news. Masters Li Chang and Xan Khan and those who accompanied them are dead."

Ma Sune pretended to be surprised. "Whoa. When, and how did this happen?"

General Chan Chou watched as one of the officers picked the head of Li Chang up and placed it inside of a clear Ziploc bag. "It happened last night at the airstrip. They were mutilated. There were other passengers as well as the pilots who were all found dead on the plane. For some reason, they weren't slaughtered in the same ruthless way as the others."

Now, it all made sense to her as to why the pilot and co-pilot never showed their faces. "So, you're saying the same murderers didn't do both killings?"

He shook his head as he continued looking at the horrific sight. "Yes, Master Ma Sune, that's exactly what I'm saying. I know Master Li Chang's work, so it's easy for me to identify the killers of the passengers and pilots. The other deaths had to be the work of the Po Clan. They are known for such ruthlessness."

Ma Sune replayed the memory in her mind. The fear she was hearing in the general's voice was pleasing. "Well, General Chan Chou, if that's the case, I'd say we have a dilemma on our hands."

As he watched the medical staff put the headless bodies inside the body bags, General Chan's expression changed from serious to fearful. "Master Ma Sune, how is your schedule for today?"

She paused, acting as if she was checking her calendar when actually she was planning something else. "I'm booked for today, General Chan." She paused again. "However, tomorrow evening before the resting of the sun my schedule will be free."

He nodded. "Great. Then we shall meet tomorrow evening to discuss the next course of action."

Ma Sune sighed. "Of course, General Chan, but first the evening rituals must be done."

Having gained the opportunity to watch, or maybe even participate, in one of the Sune Clan's rituals perked the general up. "Indeed, Master Ma Sune. I shall see you then."

Without responding, she hung up and returned to the dining table. Her hunger for food had left her and its place came the thirst for blood.

She stood behind her seat and waited for the table to be cleared before she spoke. "Kindred spirits, soon the murderers of my beloved sister, Master Khia Li Sune Po and her husband, Master Han Xi Po, will drown in his own blood right here on this compound. And this shall take place soon, tomorrow evening. Elders, Masters and Moon Tao Po, let us meet in my study immediately."

They all stood and followed Ma Sune out to her study. Inside, she closed and locked the door.

"Everyone have a seat," Ma Sune said, as she walked behind her desk and sat down. "I have great news and I realize there are questions that must be answered."

Saki raised her right hand. "Excuse me, Master Ma Sune, you are correct, and there is one serious question that must be answered. Are we going after the High Council?"

Ma Sune looked at the expressions on the faces in the room. There was no fear evident. "In due time, Master Saki Po. So, the answer to your question is *yes.* Know that the High Council would rather propose a treaty than take their chance at falling. But our overall objective is to bring an end to any and everyone responsible for the deaths of our loved ones."

Saki and everyone else nodded their approval.

"Now, for the great news," Ma Sune added and continued, "General Chan Chou will be here tomorrow evening. I have devised a plan that I think is a wonderful way to end the entire Chou Clan's legacy."

Just then, her phone rang. She pulled it out and looked at the screen. It was a private number. She answered and put the phone on speaker before sitting it on her desk. "Master Ma Sune speaking. Hello?"

A male voice came through the speaker. "Master Ma Sune, it's been awhile. This is Head Master Hia Xan Tu."

Everyone listened attentively. Ma Sune sighed and allowed the silence to linger between them for a moment before responding. "What is it you want, Head Master Hia Xan Tu?"

"To assure you the High Council had nothing to do with the actions of General Chan Chou," he replied.

"That does not excuse the deaths of Masters Khia Li Sune Po and Han Xi Po," Ma Sune said calmly. "There blood is on your hands, Head Master Hia Xan Tu. Do you deny this fact?"

Hia was had there. "I cannot say you're falsely accusing the High Council, Master Ma Sune. I know the Po and Sune Clans have reunited under the blood oath sworn by the ancestral spirits of the Black Dragon and Green Mantis. I would like to come to some kind of an agreement on your terms."

"That's an easy term, Head Master Hia Xan Tu. Stay out of our way and out of our affairs. Not to mention, there will be no more oppressing of any clan," demanded Ma Sune.

Hia sighed. "You know the High Council's decision doesn't rest upon my shoulders alone, Master Ma Sune. I shall call for an emergency vote immediately and call you back with the verdict."

He hung up. Ma Sune pressed the end call icon on her phone and leaned back in her chair. “Now we shall have our vote. Elders Mae Za Sune, Ty Po, Nam Wang Po, and Shang Sune, how shall we deal with General Chan Chou and his entire clan?”

Ty Po raised his hand and spoke his peace. “I say we allow a master of the esoteric arts of ninja deal with the Brown Locusts compound. As for General Chan Chou and those who shall accompany him here, may he suffer a thousand wounds before greeted with death, and may the shadows consume those with him.”

All of the elders nodded in agreement with Ty Po.

CHAPTER SEVEN

Head Master Hia Xan Tu called for the emergency vote. Yin Tzu, Vai Ki Hun, Chang Le, Thom Lo, Chen Sao, Mae Lin, Xul Yung, Hie Lang, Don Wu, Bolo Shang, Wen Chu, and Zhia Mi Yang sat impatiently. They all had legitimate businesses to manage during the hour but not appearing when summoned could very well mean death, according to the law of the High Council, which every member knew.

Hia walked into the council room, bowed, and took a seat. "The moment has come for this council to vote wisely. The Po and Sune Clan have reunited, and they have proposed a treaty for this council to consider. They proposed that we stay out of their affairs and that there be no oppressing of the other clans. I find their proposal reasonable, however, we must vote upon the matter. All in favor of this treaty raise your left hand."

All raised their hand with the exception of three—Don Wu, Mae Lin, and Thom Lo. Hia looked upon the three with pity. "Masters Don Wu, Mae Lin, and Thom Lo, you have been out voted considering this matter. However, if either of you would like to share your reason for not favoring the treaty, you have the right to do so."

Mae Lin stood to her feet. "I have been a member of this council for over thirty years. I was here when the Po clan decided to dishonor the contract some of their forefathers signed to be of service to the High Council. I find it dishonorable to bargain with traitors." She retook her seat.

Hia nodded. "Thank you for your honesty, Master Mae Lin. Masters Thom Lo and Don Wu, I take it your reasons are somewhat the same?"

Without words, both men nodded in the affirmative. Hia looked around the table, fully aware that three seats would have to be filled soon. "Ladies and Gentlemen, this meeting is over. You are dismissed."

Everyone stood to leave. Don Wu, Mae Lin, and Thom Lo were the first out the door.

Zhia stayed back to have a word with Hia. "Head Master Hia Xan Tu, what happens next?"

Hia looked her in the eyes. "Master Zhia Mi Yang, it's funny that you should ask. There will be three seats on this council in need of filling soon. Fate has a humorous way of dealing with certain characteristics."

Zhia nodded her understanding. "Maybe we should consider summoning masters from Po and Sune Clans to sit at the table."

Hia's eyes lit up. "Master Zhia Mi Yang, your youthfulness is a gift to this council."

She bowed and left, knowing she had found favor at the table. Hia waited until he heard the outside door close. Afterwards he proceeded to make an anticipated call. She picked up after the third ring.

He coughed to clear his throat. "Master Ma Sune, the vote is final. The High Council has voted and agreed to your terms."

"Of course, Head Master Hia Xan Tu. May we all continue to live prosperous lives," said Ma Sune.

Next, he pondered over the problem Don, Mae, and Thom would attempt to cause, so he tapped the appropriate numbers on his phone to send her a text message while she was still on the line:

> Hia: Master Ma Sune I am sending you this message as a heads up regarding a possible problem. They are the three who opposed the treaty. Here are their whereabouts. all the information needed.

He sent the text. Ma Sune received it and opened it. Speaking into the receiver she responded, "I guess we shall consider this a reassuring insurance policy of this treaty," she said as she read the text. "It'll be done on this moon, Head Master Hia Xan Tu." She hung and Hia hung up their individual lines and he relaxed in his chair.

***

Ma Sune had summoned Shyan to her study. She walked in, bowed, and remained standing. "Is there a problem, Master Ma Sune?"

Ma Sune opened the text message she'd received from the head master of the High Council before handing Shyan the phone. "Maser Shyan, have you taught anyone of the guild the arts?"

She shook her head. "No, I haven't. However, I have tutored Moon Tao Po, and she's a quick learner. Why?"

Ma Sune nodded in deep thought. "Hm . . . I see. So, what do you think about Master Sia Po? Do you think she would fare as well as Moon Tao Po?"

Shyan nodded. "Master Ma Sune, there's nothing else to be said about the matter. Consider it done." She read over the text message again before bowing and leaving. As she turned the corner, Sia and Moon came into sight.

Sia looked at her questioningly. "Master Shyan Nun Sune, what is this work you speak of?"

Not used to being asked such questions caused Shyan to sigh. "Master Sia Po, are you ready to execute true and absolute death to our enemies?"

Although she did it with slight hesitation, she nodded her willingness. "So be it Master Shyan Nun Sune. I'm ready if you're ready to teach me how."

Shyan looked at Moon. "I know I don't have to ask you. Come on. Let's go to my room. Master Malice will keep watch to make sure our bodies are not disturbed while we're gone."

The three women started for the resting quarters. Shyan explained to Sia the entire process before they made it to the room. Malice was doing a push-up and ab-routine when they entered. He took a moment to acknowledge their presence. "I haven't done anything."

Shyan shook her head. "Malice, stop being so damn comical all the time. You get to play guardian today, Mr. Freeman."

He dropped down to the floor doing push-ups. "Oh yeah? Who am I guarding?"

"Our bodies, luv," Shyan replied. "We have some pressing business to attend. You don't have to stop your little workout session. Just make sure our bodies are not disturbed."

Malice looked at the time on his Rolex. It was 11:45 am. "You all do know the afternoon ritual starts in fifteen minutes?"

Shyan shrugged her shoulders. "And? We will be back in ten minutes."

He smirked. "This means, I'm thinking you can get it done in eight."

"Come on, ladies," Shyan said to Sia and Moon, as she laid on her back on the floor. She looked in Malice's eyes before closing hers and said, "Make it seven minutes."

He sat on the floor in full lotus. As he listened, he found himself being pulled under so he quickly jumped to his feet. Within a matter of sixty seconds, the three women stood in astral form outside of their bodies.

"There are no limitations in this realm," Shyan said. "Whatever you will to do is what you *can* do. Follow me."

They traveled so fast it was as if they had entered a portal to get to their first destination. Mae Lin, her two teenage daughters, and husband were having brunch together. They had no clue of Shyan, Moon, or Sia's presence in the dining room. Shyan wielded twin short swords, Sia wielded twin daggers, and Moon wielded the short handle sickles.

Without hesitation, they ripped their spirits away from their souls and severed the cord that kept the spirit attached to the body. Mae Lin and her household died without a fighting chance. Not willing to waste time, Shyan revealed to Sia and Moon another aspect of the astral realm. And before they knew it, they found themselves standing on the front lawn of Thom Lo's estate. Then, the three women disappeared and reappeared inside the main house where Thom Lo was seemed to be enjoying himself with three teenage prostitutes.

Shyan turned to face Sia and Moon. "There is no time for mercy. No one survives."

Moon and Sia nodded, and the three shadow walkers went to work.

Sia thrust the twin daggers through the flesh of one of the naked women and pulled her spirit from her body before destroying it completely. Moon ripped the spirits from the other two girls' bodies at the same time with the ethereal blades. After she had snatched them out of the physical forms that housed them, she cut the spirits asunder, dispersing the energy to become nothingness.

Seeing the three teenage girls' bodies collapse, Thom Lo panicked. But before he could scream, Shyan thrust one of the ethereal blades through his heart while slashing clean through his neck with the other, causing him to collapse on top of one of the girls. "Two down," she said, "and one to go. Let's finish this, so we can return to our physical forms."

The three mercenaries disappeared and materialized in Don Wu's driveway. Shyan realized they were right on time because he and his wife were getting in the car. "We shall wait right here," she said, as the car came towards them.

As the car passed through them, Shyan, Sia, and Moon's blades pierced Don Wu and his wife's souls and claimed the lives of their spirits. The car veered off the driveway and struck a tree.

"Disperse of your weapons and take ahold of my hand," demanded Shyan.

Sia and Moon did as they were instructed. And as soon as they grabbed her hand, they found themselves opening their physical eyes. When Shyan looked at Malice he nodded. "Impressive, Mrs. Freeman. You actually did it in six minutes and thirty three seconds."

She stood up and helped Sia to her feet. "Another normal day of life, Malice. Thanks for not coming along with us."

"I damn near did," he said. He chuckled and rubbed his head.

"But you didn't," she replied.

He looked at the time. "Well, it's time for the afternoon rituals." He looked at Sia, who seemed a little tired. "Master Sia Po, are you going to make it or do you need to rest?"

Remembering it was her day to lead, Sia shook the tiredness off. "I'm okay. Let's go."

Together, Malice, Shyan, Moon, and Sia, left the sleeping quarters and walked out into the courtyard. Everyone else was already sitting quietly in meditation when they arrived. Shyan, Malice, and Moon took their places in the ranks.

Once Sia reached the platform, everyone stood to their feet. She performed a graceful bow before facing toward the opposite direction and beginning the ritual. Her movements were easy to follow. She moved with the grace and nimbleness of a professional dancer. The transition through every element began and ended at its highest peak.

All of a sudden, Sia changed tempo. Her emotions became heightened by the emotions within the elements. No one was able to keep up at the speed she performed the chaotic state of every element, so they stopped and watched. The sight before them had them in awe.

As Sia continued to transition through the emotional state of Nature, a sand funnel started forming about her. The stronger the emotion she displayed in the transition, the thicker the sand funnel became. It circled and whirled about her at such a speed, it became impossible for anyone to see through it. But they knew Sia was at the center, controlling the cyclone.

Ma Sune raised her left hand high above her head. When she made a fist, the Green Mantises began throwing series after series of ninja stars toward the cyclone. As she had suspected, it was an impenetrable forcefield. The thrown instruments of death found their way into the sand outside of the cyclone.

Finally, Sia found her peace. Her emotions became calm and the cyclone of sand receded. Once the sand had settled again, she prostrated, stood and bowed. She walked off the platform to stand in the ranks next to Saki and Yishi.

Saki nodded admiringly. "Master Sia Po, the Black Dragon Spirit within has taken full control."

Sia continued to look straight ahead. "Yes, Master Saki. The arcane arts of Ninja unlocks doorways within, I've never felt better."

Ma Sune stood on the platform and bowed. "Masters Shyan Nun Sune and Sia Po, and Moon Tao Po, please join me at my side."

They filed out of the ranks and walked onto the platform. Ma Sune bowed to each one individually before addressing the clans. “Kindred spirits, take a good look at the three mighty warriors standing here. They are true shadow walkers. The spirit of Ninja courses through their being. They are to be honored as masters.”

Everyone bowed to show their respect to Shyan, Sia, and Moon. All three women bowed in return. Ma Sune continued to speak. “Again, we have witnessed another powerful aspect of our blood oath. Now, let us go prepare for the noon meal.”

Everyone left, taking in casual conversations on their way to freshen up. Moon entered her room to find Jennifer lounging in her panties and bra watching television and eating. Without saying a word, Moon grabbed a change of under garments and clothes and went straight to the shower. Once done, she stepped back into the room fully dressed.

The kitchen helper knocked, and Jennifer opened the door. She handed the helper the dirty dishes and thanked her. She bowed and left. Jennifer closed and locked the door. She realized nobody ever smiled and they all looked at her with distrust and dislike in their eyes.

She walked back over to the bed and dove onto it. She propped her head up and stared at Moon. “Tabby, where are you off to now?”

Moon looked in the mirror, tying her hair into a ponytail. “To do exactly what you just finished doing, Jenn. Unlike you, I have obligations to fulfill.”

Jennifer sucked her teeth. “Whose fault is that? You haven't had time for me since we left Jersey. Not to mention, everyone around here seems to dislike me or trust me.”

Moon laughed. “Jenn, if you knew some real history you would understand that not many people of color really like or trust your people.”

Jennifer frowned. “What in the hell is that supposed to mean, Tabby? This is my first and last time coming to China. I've never been to Africa or anywhere in the islands.”

"But you've been to and live in America," Moon cut her off saying, "and that was another cruel and ruthless moment in history." She eyed Jennifer through the mirror. "And not to rain in on your parade, but the apple never falls too far from the tree."

Jennifer became outraged. "You know what? Fuck you Tabitha Greene! I knew I was making a mistake messing with you!"

Moon turned around with a smile on her face. "See what I mean? All of you are driven by your lusts to be in control and have power over others." She unlocked and opened the door and didn't bother to close it when she left.

Filled with anger, Jennifer got up and slammed the door. *I'll be glad when this is all over so I can go back to my normal life and be done with all of you*, she thought to herself, as she resumed watching television.

***

General Chan and a squadron of officers were at the crime scene. One of the neighbors had called and reported it after going to check on the Lin family. Not seeing any visible wounds, they noticed there was a little blood from the nose of each victim. General Chan knew it wasn't an ordinary cause of death, and when he looked in the face of Mae Lin, he was overcome by fear. Before him lay a dead member of the High Council.

He took out his phone and nervously dialed the head master's number. The phone rang twice before he picked up. "What is it, General Chan Chou? I thought I made myself clear that the High Council will have no part in this little personal vendetta of yours."

"I was calling to inform you that Master Mae Lin and her family is dead. Me and my men are on the scene now. And I can tell you, this was the work of the dark arts," Chan said. His voice trembled nervously.

Hia sighed. "And you shall find the same for Masters Thom Lo and Don Wu. The High Council isn't invincible General Chan Chou."

He hung up. General Chan ordered his men to come with him. “Let the medical personnel handle this mess,” he told them.

They hopped in the government issued vehicles. With the sirens blaring, they sped to Don Wu's home. The general immediately noticed the car crashed against a tree and sent one of his men to check things out on the rest of the premises.

The man opened the car door on the passenger side and checked their pulse. Spotting the dried blood under their noses, the officer walked back over to the squad car shaking his head. “They're dead, sir.”

General Chan nodded in deep thought. “Was there anything that might suggest the murders are somehow linked?”

“Yes, sir,” the officer replied. “The same nose bleed. Plus, there are no visible puncture wounds or cause of death.”

“Great work, officer,” Chan complimented. “Radio for the medics and get in. We have one more place to check out.”

The officer radioed for the medics and got in the front passenger seat. General Chan floored the vehicle. The other squad cars followed his lead. While on the way, he redialed the head master's number.

“General Chan Chou,” Hia began when he answered, “are you calling me because you are afraid?”

“I'm calling you trying to figure out what the hell is going on,” Chan replied.

“General, the day of reckoning comes to us all when we choose to go against the grain so to speak. You awaken the dragon, so it's your responsibility to put it back to sleep.”

Chan laughed nervously. “As if that's an easy task, Head Master Hia Xan Tu. I need more support.”

Hia sighed his usual sigh. “If you really value my advice, I suggest you take the rest of the day off. Go home, General Chan Chou, and spend time with your family. You never know when the Angel of death will come.”

The headmaster hung up. General Chan tossed his phone onto the dashboard. They were driving up the driveway of Thom Lo's estate. He skidded to a stop in front of the main house and jumped out. Followed by his men, he ran inside the house after kicking the front door in. He told them to spread out and search the house. Upon approaching the master bedroom, one of his men radioed them to come up. There, lying on top of a dead and naked teenage girl, was a dead Thom Lo.

Chan shook his head uncertain of what else to do. The sight of the three teenage girls' naked corpses were images that would be branded within his mind forever. And then there was the look of horror and fear frozen on Thom Lo's face—all of which added to the dread he was already feeling.

***

After the noon meal, Ma Sune, Yishi, Saki, Nya, Sia, Moon, Malice, Shyan, Trent, Mae Za Sune, Ty Po, Nam Wang Po, and Shang Sune met in the courtyard.

Ma Sune was ready to reveal her plan for the following evening. "Masters Shyan Nun Sune, Sia Po, and Moon Tao Po, Master Shyan Nun Sune already knows what is expected of you all tomorrow. You all have had a busy day, so you're excused for the remainder of this day. The evening meal will be delivered to your resting quarters."

They bowed and left the courtyard. Ma Sune turned her attention to Malice and Trent. "Guild Masters, you are in charge of the deaths of those who will be accompanying General Chan Chou tomorrow evening. By all means, deal with them as you see fit."

After addressing them, she turned her full attention to Saki, Yishi, Nya, and the elders. "You all shall be the only ones attending the evening ritual. We shall give General Chan Chou a ceremonial death."

Ma Sune explained in detail, her plans. Every one of the elders nodded, giving their approval.

"Now that we all know the tasks before us, let's enjoy the rest of our day," said Ma Sune, before bowing and walking off.

Malice and Trent lagged behind. After everyone was out of earshot, Trent turned to him and asked, "So, when is the big day?"

"Probably a week after tomorrow," Malice replied, after he'd thought for a moment. I have to make the proper arrangements with Mae Za Sune."

Trent nodded. "So, how are we going to deal with the situation tomorrow? What's the plan?"

Malice grinned. "Tomorrow, we will be Green Mantises for the entire day."

Trent smiled, liking the element of surprise. "This will be done quietly and quickly. I guess I'll see your face for the last time at dinner until this is over."

He nodded. "Likewise, my brother. Let's go enjoy the rest of our day." The two master mercenaries walked out of the courtyard.

Ma Sune sat in her study in deep thought. To finally have come to the truth of what happened to her sister, Khia, lifted a burdensome weight off of her heart. To know that she was about to slaughter the his entire family along with the men who were all responsible for Khia's death, made her feel that much more at peace. A vengeful kind of peace, to say the least.

Nya was in her room sharpening the blades of her personal swords. She couldn't help but think about the past. The day when she and her two sisters, Ma and Khia, stood in the courtyard ready to prove themselves worthy of being Green Mantises. It was one of her best memories. . .

There they were at twelve years old, Khia, Ma, and Nya, all dressed in the forest green ceremonial wear standing before the whole Sune Clan. Their mother, Mae Za Sune, and father, Dae Lue Sune, stood in the front of the ranks.

"My daughters," said Mae Za Sune, "today you prove yourselves as descendants of the spirit of the Green Mantis. Are you ready?"

They all bowed and nodded silently. Without saying a word, Mae Za Sune gave a simple nod of her head, giving the signal for the ceremony to begin. Khia, Ma, and Nya stood back-to-back, but quickly found themselves diving, tucking, and rolling on the sand to evade the assault of the ninja stars being thrown at them. They weren't given time to get back to their feet. The projectiles continued to come their way, so they continued to roll left and right to avoid death.

After the stars ceased to come at them maliciously, Nya, Khia, and Ma regrouped and stood back-to-back. All of a sudden, Nya heard the sound of a dart. Right in the nick of time, she caught the dart between her fingers seconds before it would've made contact with Nya's face. As she threw the dart to the sand, more of them began to fly in their direction.

As they back dropped to the sand and rolled over onto their stomachs, Khia caught a glimpse of the Green Mantises movement. She pointed in the directions the darts had come from. Nya and Ma looked and nodded. Ma Sune, having always been determined to prove herself, scrambled to her feet and went for the target closest to her.

When she reached her target, she latched onto the assassin and with all her strength, dropped back, and followed with a leg toss. The Green Mantis struck back first into the sand. She rolled over on top of her target and struck him twice in the face. The ninja yielded before she let him up.

Khia went for the opponent farthest away. She found herself having to dive forward in the air to evade one of the deadly darts, before rolling right back to her feet. Just as she was about to reach him, she came to an abrupt stop and turned sideways to avoid getting killed by another oncoming dart. Afterwards, she rushed forward.

She reached the disguised assassin and struck him with a knife hand strike to the stomach. As he doubled over forward, she grabbed him around the neck and rolled backwards. Before she struck him again, he bowed out of the fight.

Nya had exposed the last disguised Green Mantis. She caught him with a thrust kick to the stomach before striking him down with a dragon knee to the face.

"Halt!" yelled their father in Chinese.

Nya and her sisters stood together before their clan and bowed. The emotion in their parents' eyes was filled with pride and delight. They had proved themselves worthy to their clan. . .

Nya finished sharpening the steel blades. All she could think about was the pleasure she was going to feel having the blood of her sister's murderer stain her blades.

***

General Chan had taken the head master's advice. He took the rest of the day off to be with his wife and four sons. Although his sons seemed happy to have him around, his wife didn't. She seemed distracted by her own thoughts.

After dinner, his sons let he and his wife know they were going to the arcades to play videogames with their friends. Sensing the distance from his wife, that gave him some time alone with her. Chan made an attempt to touch and kiss her, though she evaded his touch and stopped his kisses.

He looked at her, feeling offended. “Sue Chou, what is your problem?”

She stared at him in disbelief. “Chan, are you serious right now? I do watch the news you know.”

“What is that supposed to mean,” he shot back.

Sue sighed out of frustration. “For the sake of our family Chan, you need to let go of your pride and ego. Your little private war with the Po Clan is the cause of the recent lives that have been taken. How many more lives are you willing to sacrifice, Chan Chou?”

His expression turned cold. “This will all be over soon, Sue.”

She shook her head and laughed sarcastically. “General Chan Chou, you are mad. What clan has ever opposed the Po Clan and survived to speak of it? None,” she said answering her own question, “because no clan is stupid enough to get their own family slaughtered,” she concluded. Her tone reflected her disgust with the situation.

He reached at her a second time, only to get his head slapped away. “Don't touch me. As a matter of fact, I don't want you to even *think* about touching me until you come to your senses, Chan Chou. Hopefully, that will be before death finds us all.”

Chan didn't try forcing the issue. He walked out, jumped in his car, and left. He found himself driving down the strip where prostitution was the main attraction. He pulled over on the side and waited for one to approach his car.

He watched as a Caucasian woman, wearing a blonde wig, approached the passenger side door. She leaned over in the window, smiling. “Hi there, daddy. Are you looking for a great time?”

“Get in,” he told her and flashed a wad of yens.

The lady didn't hesitate to hop in the passenger’s seat.

“Where to, daddy? If you want, we can do it right here.” She rubbed his manhood through his pants. “Right now,” she added, with lust dripping from her tone.

Feeling his nature rising, he put the car in drive and drove off. “We’ll be getting a room because I want your company all night.”

“No problem,” she replied

The drive to the hotel was quick and quiet. He gave her the money to go pay for the room and waited in the car until she returned with the room key. When she returned, they hurried to the room and locked the door after hanging a do-no-disturb sign on the outside.

“Now, what will it be first, daddy,” the prostitute asked. She began taking off the skimpy clothes and underwear she’d worn.

Chan undressed himself and sat naked on the edge of the bed. “Come make your money by making me happy, baby.”

She walked over to him and got down on her knees in submission to his request. Looking into his eyes, she grabbed hold of his cock and began stroking it up and down until it became erect. Then she descended upon it, wrapping her lips around him. She bobbed up and down the full length of his erection, causing him to moan while grabbing a fist full of her hair.

After so long, he pulled her head up and told her to get on top. She obeyed and eased down the full length of his manliness before bucking on top of him like a wild stallion. He held on and buried his face between her bouncing large soft breasts. He didn't even care to warn her of his oncoming release, instead, he filled her insides up to the brim.

She continued to bounce up and down on his lap without remorse and yelled as she released around his sex. The feel of her warm pleasure caused him to become aroused again. He commanded her to get off of him, and to get on her knees on the bed and bend over. She did exactly as she'd been told.

She gasped as he entered her anally. Without compassion, he pounded away inside of her. She screamed at the top of her lungs due to the combination of pain and pleasure. When her anal began to cream over, the sensation from the slippery wetness caused him to pound harder and deeper inside her. Just as his second release approached, he pulled out of her anus and slid inside her vagina.

Chan short-stroked her, hard and fast. Even after he had cum inside of her yet again, he continued until his tool was back to its upright, elevated position. They screwed one another's brains out until neither of them could go any longer. The prostitute sat up on the side of the bed and fired up a cigarette.

She took a puff and looked at him with a smile plastered on her face. "Daddy, I'll be sure to give you my personal number. You can call on me any time," she offered.

Chan lay on his back staring at the ceiling. "You're definitely a lot of fun girl. Let's get a little rest, so we can go another round before morning.

She finished her cigarette and lay down beside him. They fell asleep almost immediately.

CHAPTER EIGHT

Morning came quicker than what Moon Tao Po had hoped for. And the position she'd found herself in definitely wasn't what she'd hoped for. Jennifer rubbed and kissed on her. She slid her hand between Moon's thighs and began rubbing on her sex.

She laid her naked body on top of Moon and began sliding up and down. She moaned and pressed harder against her until her body relaxed with the flow of her release.

Moon Tao Po stared at the ceiling, feeling like she'd had just been raped. The thought itself angered her to the point that she pushed Jennifer off of her.

Jennifer looked at her with defiance. "What the hell is wrong with you, Tabitha? What, I'm not good enough for you anymore since you've become such an expert killer?"

Moon jumped out of bed and went to the bathroom with Jennifer hot on her heels. "So, it's back to the silent treatment, huh?"

Moon didn't respond. She ignored her by brushing her teeth, but her actions didn't deter Jennifer from talking. "You people and your dumb ass rules."

Her comment caused Tabitha to halt. She stopped brushing her teeth and looked at Jennifer with a look Jennifer had never seen her display. Her eyes radiated a nonverbal warning, but of course, she didn't take heed. "Tabitha, I know you hear me talking to you."

She proceeded to finish brushing her teeth, quickly and in silence, before washing her face.

"Y'all niggers and chinks are all the same," Jennifer belted out, out of anger. She knew she had gone too far, but she'd said it, and it was too late to take it back now.

Before Moon could catch herself, she shot Jennifer a straight-stiff right jab to the chin that knocked her out cold. Leaving the bathroom, she stepped right over her unconscious body. After getting dressed, she walked out of the room without checking to see if she was alright.

On the way down the hall, she passed by the kitchen helper, who always took Jennifer her meals. In passing, they bowed to one another in respectfully.

Moon entered the dining hall and realized her usual seat across from Sia had been taken by Yuri, but there was a seat open next to Sia and Shyan. The cooks and kitchen help waiting patiently at the kitchen doors carted the meal in as soon as she sat down. She looked around the table and noticed Malice and Trent weren't in sight, nevertheless, she thought nothing of it. The morning meal was served, and everyone ate their share.

After the table was cleared, Mae Za Sune stood to her feet and spoke. "Kindred spirits, especially my daughters and grandchildren, this sun is indeed a glorious light shining upon us. Before the moon and stars reveals the heavens, the murderers of Masters Khia Li Sune Po and Han Xi Po blood will stain our blades and soak into the sand beneath our feet. The spirits of the Black Dragon and Green Mantis shall find peace in the blood sacrifice offered this sun. It serves as a new constitution signed in the blood of our enemies, of the blood oath." She bowed and returned to her seat.

Ma Sune stood and looked around the table in deep thought. "This sun is the Sun of reckoning. There will only be one ritual performed this sun, and it is the death of the Brown Locust." She looked at Yuri. "Yuri, you, and two Green Mantises shall be the welcoming party this evening."

He sprang to his feet, feeling honored to be given such a task. "As you wish, Master Ma Sune." He bowed and returned to his seat.

"Enjoy your day," said Ma Sune, before walking out followed by Yishi, Saki, and Nya.

Before they could step outside, the kitchen helper who delivered the food to Jennifer hurried over to Ma Sune but kept her eyes on Moon Tao Po. "Master Ma Sune, may I have a word with you and Master Moon Tao Po?"

Ma Sune nodded. "Of course, Myka." She looked over to where Shyan, Sia, and Moon stood talking and called for them to come over. They dropped whatever conversation they were having and joined Ma Sune and the others. "Let's take a walk," Ma Sune said.

They walked outside. They continued to walk in silence until they came upon Yuri training with the three chain linked Bo staff. They stopped and watched him wield the weapon to perfection.

"Yuri has been training with that weapon since he was first able to pick it up," Yishi commented. "But we're not here to talk about Yuri's weapon proficiency. What is this matter you would like to speak of, Myka?"

Myka bowed and looked at Moon. "When I entered Master Moon Toa Po's room to serve the guest her meal, I found her unconscious on the bathroom floor."

"Did you check to see if she was still alive, or attempt to help her, Myka," Yishi asked?

Myka shook her head. "No, I did not, Master Yishi. I wouldn't dare dishonor the ancestral spirit by assisting a demon. I simply left the tray on the table and exited the room."

"Good," Yishi said coldly.

Ma Sune had to stifle a laugh before speaking. "So, Master Moon Tao Po, what happened?"

Remembering Jennifer's exact words, her facial expression turned cold. "Everyone, please forgive me for the words I'm about to use. But if I'm to speak the truth, then I must repeat exactly what Jennifer said about us. Her exact words were, "'y'all niggers and chinks are all the same.'"

All of the women gasped. Moon continued. "Upon Jennifer's racist statement being made, I, without hesitation, or regret, knocked her out with a stiff right jab to the chin and left her lying on the floor of the bathroom."

They all stood, looking shocked and taken aback. Though not surprised. A few even thinking of a more malicious way to kill Jennifer. Although Saki and Shyan knew something that the others didn't, they were still having thoughts of ending her life.

Myka was so upset she just had to speak her mind. "I would be honored if you would allow me to poison the demon," she said coldly.

Shyan was always one to think things through. She shook her head. "No, that won't be necessary, Myka. She's in the hands of death at all times. Let's stay focused on the true prize of this sun." She looked at Moon and bowed. "Master Moon Tao Po, you have served justice by not allowing our culture and people to be disrespected. You are worthy to be called my sister."

Saki, Yishi, Ma, Nya, and Myka nodded in agreement with Shyan. Even Yuri, who had overheard their conversation, stopped training and bowed. "And Master Moon Tao Po, you are my sister and cousin as well."

Moon bowed back to Yuri before they started their walk towards Ma Sune's study. Noon was approaching fast, and they were anticipating the moment.

Jennifer opened her eyes in pain. She was still dazed so she used the bathroom sink to pull herself up. Looking in the mirror, she noticed the dark bruise on her chin. The last thing she remembered was arguing with Tabitha. *That black bitch*, she thought to herself. She touched her chin and winced, feeling the soreness. She couldn't wait to get back to the states so she could get her revenge. She knew she couldn't beat Tabitha physically, but she would use the federal agency to get back at her.

She splashed cold water onto her face to shake off the dizziness. She had made up her mind. She would demand that they allow her to leave immediately on a flight before the day was over. And when she got home, she would use the agency to destroy Tabitha and their entire ring of murderers.

She didn't bother taking a shower. She got dressed and stormed out of the room, determined to get her way. She found her way outside after wandering around for ten minutes. She stopped everyone she came in contact with and asked if they knew where she could find Tabitha, but no one seemed to know who Tabitha was.

Jennifer's anger was starting to get the best of her when she thought of Saki and Sia. She walked out into an opening, where she saw a little boy training with his weapon. She stepped over to him, staying out of reach of the weapon. "Excuse me."

Yuri looked at her and continued his training. "What do you want?" he asked coldly, not even attempting to hide his dislike.

She smiled nervously. "Can you show me where I can find Master Saki or Sia Po right now?"

"Yes, but no," he answered without a hint of politeness.

Jennifer was getting frustrated. She took out some U.S. dollars. "Okay then. How much is it going to cost me for your assistance?"

Yuri's demeanor turned colder. "I'm not your slave demon." Without hesitation, he swept her off her feet with the Bo staff. Just as he was about to strike Jennifer in the head, Yishi ran out of the study followed by Ma Sune, Saki, Sia, Shyan, Nya, and Moon.

"Stand down, Yuri," Yishi commanded in Chinese.

"This demon tried to buy me like I am a slave," Yuri said in Chinese while holding the end of the Bo staff a couple inches away from Jennifer's throat.

She sighed, shaking her head. She was wrestling with her thoughts. Part of her wanted to tell Yuri to kill her. *But that would be even crueler to him than her,* she thought to herself. She and the others walked over to them. "Stand down, Yuri," she repeated in a more demanding tone.

Hesitantly, he stepped back a few paces. Yishi didn't give anyone else a chance to speak. She handled the matter as she saw fit. Looking down at Jennifer she said, "Get up. Don't expect anyone to help you up."

Jennifer got to her feet quickly. "I'm not here to start any trouble."

Yishi looked her up and down. "That's what you say. What do you want?"

"I want— No, I demand to leave this hell hole and be on a flight back home today," she replied.

Yishi looked around. "I don't hear anyone protesting your demand, Jennifer. If it was left up to me, you would've never set foot on this compound. Gather your belongings and leave. Nobody's going to stop you. Trust me."

Jennifer looked at Tabitha. "Tabitha, are you coming with me?"

Yishi smirked. "Who is Tabitha? There's no one here named Tabitha."

Jennifer then took two steps towards Moon Tao Po and found herself being cut off by Sia who didn't say a word.

But Yishi, on the other hand did. "I have told you as nicely as I can to gather your things and leave. Don't get yourself involved in trouble you won't make it out of."

Jennifer looked past Sia at Tabitha with hatred in her eyes. "That's what's up, Tabitha. I'm leaving. You best believe I'm going to have the last laugh."

She stormed off in the direction of the sleeping quarters. Shyan shook her head with pity before going after her. "Jennifer, wait a second."

She stopped and turned around, facing Shyan with tears in her eyes. "Don't you try to stop me, Angel. I'm done with her."

Shyan looked at her sideways. "Oh, I'm not the one to try and stop you from doing anything. As far as I'm concerned, Yuri could've bashed your face in until he killed you."

Jennifer looked at her and frowned. "At least you're honest and real about your feelings. Anyway, what did you stop me for?"

Shyan leaned closely and whispered in her left ear. "You're dying, Jennifer. Hopefully, you'll make it back to Jersey and begin some cancer treatment."

Jennifer's eyes widened from fear. "What?"

Shyan stood backed up. "You heard me. Your clock is ticking. Goodbye. Hopefully, we don't cross paths again, Jennifer."

Jennifer turned around and hurried inside to pack her things. *Oh, but we will, Angel, and all of you are going down*, she thought to herself, as she continued to pack. She finished packing and walked out. Yishi and Saki escorted her to the front gates and stood watch until she was in a cab and gone.

***

Chan was up getting the final service before check out time. He released inside of the prostitute again and again without a care in the world. She was back on top, taking him for the ride of his life when he thought about what he had to do. He looked at the time. It was almost eleven o'clock, and he had a few stops to make before meeting with Ma Sune.

He grabbed her hips and pumped inside of her hard and fast until he came inside of her. He felt her release flow with his.

She got up and started getting dressed. “Big Daddy, you been nuttin’ inside of me all this time. I'm not on shots or the pills, so you've taken a chance on getting me pregnant.”

Chan put on his clothes. “So. As long as you're my personal call girl, I don't care.” He handed her the wad of money he'd flashed the night before. “This should hold you over until I call you again. Right now, I’ve got business to take care of.”

He left the prostitute sitting on the bed in the hotel room. Once he’d made it to his car, he hopped in and drove off, feeling like a heavy weight had been lifted off him. He made it to the station and took a shower in the weight room shower. He put on the uniform he kept in his office just for occasions like this one. Feeling unusually good about himself, he picked up his phone and made a couple of important phone calls before calling home to talk to his wife.

She answered on the fourth ring. “Hello?”

“Hello, Sue Chou. How're you and the boys?” he asked.

“Fine,” she replied in a flat tone.

Chan sighed, realizing she was still upset. “That's good to know. I was just calling to let you know I won't be home again tonight.

“Okay,” she responded, right before hanging up.

General Chan wanted so badly to call her back and give her a verbal lashing, but he knew it would be a waste of time and words. Instead, he called to have his personal guards meet him outside the station around five. After that was settled, he leaned back in his chair and watched the clock on the wall. It was two o'clock pm.

As he relaxed, he had another thought hit him. He sat up straight in his chair, picked up the phone off the desk, and called Ma Sune. She answered right away. “Good afternoon, General Chan Chou.”

“Good afternoon, Master Ma Sune,” he replied. “I was calling to make sure nothing had come up that might have negated our meeting.”

“No, nothing has come up, General Chan,” she said.

Chan grinned. “Well, Master Ma Sune, that’s great to know. I shall see you soon.”

“Of course,” she replied and hung up.

He hung up and relaxed, leaning back in the chair once again. Everything was going as planned. *Soon, I will be the headmaster of the High Council*, he thought to himself.

***

The High Council was back in session. Everyone except Hia and Zhia took notice of the three empty seats. They knew Thom, Mae, and Don were dead, so neither of them stared out of curiosity. In fact, seeing the empty seats brought about feelings of fear because it was a true revelation of how easy it must’ve been to have their entire family killed.

Discerning the reality of it all, Vai Ki Hun spoke her peace. “Head Master and Masters, I'm not even going to state the tragedy which has befallen on Masters Mae Lin, Thom Lo, and Don Wu. This council was birthed to maintain a balance within the way of ninja. The dishonorable deaths of Masters Khia Li Sune Po and Han Xi Po tilted this balance, and now we are all witnessing the effects there of. I propose a vote to leave the three seats vacant until the spirits of the Black Dragon and Green Mantis find peace.” Master Vai Ki Hun sat back down.

Hia nodded. “Master Vai Ki Hun has brought to light a matter of importance. Some of you might not be familiar with the blood oath sworn to by Po and Sune clan. Not to go into detail, but I will tell you this much, they are the superior clans when it comes to warriors and the way of ninja. Together, they are undefeatable and invincible. With that being said, all in favor of Master Vai Ki Hun's proposal, raise your left hand.”

All hands went up without hesitation. Hia nodded his approval. “Master Vai Ki Hun, your proposal is approved. The three empty seats of this council shall remain empty until further notice.”

Hia looked around the table to see if anyone else had anything to say. When the silence remained undisturbed, he dismissed them.

***

Instead of going straight to the airport, Jennifer instructed the cab driver to take her to the embassy. As she got out with her luggage, she paid the tab and told him he didn't have to wait for her. Thinking about what Angel had told her, she took a deep breath and sighed before walking into the federal building. She flashed her federal badge and identified herself to the receptionist.

"Yes, and how may I help you, ma'am," the lady asked, after entering Jennifer's federal badge number in the computer, and pulling up her file.

Jennifer did her best to maintain a professional mannerism. "I've been diagnosed with having some form of cancer. I need immediate testing to be sure of the accuracy of my diagnosis. If it's accurate, I'm requesting to start treatment now and an emergency evac chopper to fly me back to the U.S. immediately."

The receptionist picked up the phone and dialed the number of the embassy's medical clinic. Jennifer stood a little impatient and listened to the one side of the conversation she could hear.

"Yes, I have Federal Agent Jennifer here at the front desk. She needs immediate medical attention. Okay. Yes, ma'am."

Before the receptionist could hang up, a team of medical personnel came bursting through a set of doors with a stretcher and an IV bag.

The doctor approached Jennifer. "Agent, I'm Doctor William Hadley. Let's get you on the stretcher and taken care of."

She laid down on the stretcher and one of the nurses inserted the needle into her right arm to start the IV. The doctor asked one of the military officers to secure her properly, before they rushed her back through the double doors and into the medical facility. They took blood samples and started running tests immediately.

Doctor Hadley returned to her bedside with an iPod in his hands. "Agent Jennifer, when were you originally diagnosed?" the doctor asked, while typing in his password.

She laughed nervously, thinking about what Angel had whispered into her ear. “Doctor Hadley, this may sound odd to you, but I was just told this information hours ago.”

He looked at the test results on the screen. “Well, whoever told you this just saved your life.” He turned the screen so she could see it, while he pointed and explained. “Those are cancerous tumors. Your immune system has kept them from attaching themselves to an organ.”

The color that had drained from Jennifer's face at the beginning of the conversation slowly returned. “So, what are you actually telling me, Doctor Hadley?”

“We can remove the tumors out of your uterus right here, without any complications,” he replied. “That's if you give the consent.”

Jennifer nodded. “Come on with the paper work for me to sign.”

“Thankfully, the world is predominantly electronic.” He pulled up the consent form on the iPad. “Sign the form there, electronically, and initial it there, and we're ready to go.”

She didn't even take the time to read it. She signed the form and handed him the iPad.

He smiled. “Let's get you fixed up. The procedure will only take up to two hours. After you've rested for a couple of hours, we'll get you in the air heading home.”

The doctor stood and began giving orders. His smile was the last thing Jennifer saw before the medicine, injected into the IV tube by the nurse, ran its course through her vein. She was out like a light.

***

Zhia Mi Yang found herself in her office on the docks. She was reading through business proposals from several independent companies within the immediate area. She came across a document with Sune's Fabric Industries circling about the logo of a green praying mantis. Seeing Ma Sune's name at the bottom of the document, Zhia's curiosity got the best of her.

She read the proposal to expand Sune's Fabric Industries through her shipping company. The percentage Zhia would receive off of all sales and distribution was considerable. So considerable she picked up the phone and called the contact number on the document. Someone answered immediately.

"Hello," said Ma Sune. "This is Ma Sune. How might I help you?"

"Master Ma Sune, this is Zhia Mi Yang. "I've just read your proposal, and I'm highly considering taking you up on your offer."

"So, when would you like to meet to discuss business, Master Zhia Mi Yang," asked Ma Sune?

Zhia looked at the calendar on her desk. "I'm free now if you're available."

Ma Sune sighed. "Master Zhia Mi Yang, you of all people know I won't be available today. Did you not recently take a seat at the council table?"

Zhia was surprised, but not shocked by how informed Ma Sune was. "Master Ma Sune, it would be foolish to lie to such a well-informed person. We shall conclude our business after you have completed the task you have set in motion."

"As you have spoken, Master Zhia Mi Yang," she replied. "I look forward to having a healthy business relationship with you."

"And, I, with you," Zhia said. "Goodbye, Master Ma Sune." Zhia disconnected the call.

She reached inside of the top left drawer of the desk and pulled out an ink casing and opened it. She read over Ma Sune's proposal again. Satisfied, she stamped it as confirmed and put her signature on the document. *Never know when you may need such a business partner,* she thought to herself. She decided not to even bother with waiting. She faxed the document to Ma Sune with a short note stating don't worry about a meeting. Our business relationship starts immediately.

***

It was 4:35 p.m. when General Chan's phone vibrated against his upper left thigh, waking him out of his sleep. “Boy, she really put it on me,” he said to himself, as he pulled out his iPhone and answered.

“We're outside in front of the station waiting on you, sir,” the caller said.

The general looked at the time on the phone and jumped to his feet. “I'm on my way out now.”

He hung up the phone and tossed it on the desk. “Won't be needing you for the rest of the day,” he said to himself. But then he thought about a little victory celebration with the prostitute afterwards and grabbed the phone and headed out.

General Chan walked through the station all smiles. He bowed to everyone he passed on the way out. He stood on the steps and brushed down the front of his service coat to smooth over the wrinkles, before walking over to the waiting car with tinted windows. He got in on the rear passenger side.

“The Sune Estate,” said General Chan.

The driver nodded and pulled off, followed by another car with the same mirror tint. They pulled into the flow of traffic. Chan, feeling the need to call Ma Sune to inform her that he was in route to her, took out his phone and called. She picked up immediately.

“General Chan, I'm guessing this phone call is to let me know you're on the way,” said Ma Sune.

He continued to smile. “Correct you are, Master Ma Sune,” He was about to hang up when he thought about the three High Council members. “Master Ma Sune, I almost forgot to inform you of the deaths of three members of the High Council and their families.”

“Well, that's less we have to concern ourselves with, General Chan,” she said coldly, before hanging up.

And she's right, Chan thought to himself, as he turned his phone completely off and sat it on the seat next to him. He wasn't about to let anything interrupt the meeting.

***

Ma Sune, Shyan, Sia, and Moon sat in her study. They'd just listened to the general confirm over the phone that he was on his way. It was the confirmation Shyan had waited patiently to hear. She, along with Sia and Moon, excused themselves and walked over to her room.

Inside, Shyan asked Moon to lock the door, and she instructed Sia to grab three comforters and pillows to spread out on the floor. Once that was done, she lit three scented candles and turned off the lights. As the three women laid down on the floor, Shyan asked Sia and Moon if they needed a guide. Each replied, *"No."*

"Masters Sia and Moon, remember, no one is to survive," Shyan reminded them, before they entered the astral realm.

CHAPTER NINE

Shyan, Sia, and Moon materialized near the front gates of the Brown Locusts' compound. Moon Tao Po wielded her favorite weapon, two short handle sickles. She quickly severed the life cords within the three Brown Locusts at the gate with one swing. They fell to the ground lifeless. With that done, the three ruthless mercenaries walked through the closed gates.

"First, we spread out and sweep the perimeter. Then we shall meet up within the house. We will go through every room, and if there be any life inside, destroy it," commanded Shyan, before taking off at the speed of light.

Sia wielded the twin ethereal daggers and disappeared. She reappeared at the rear of the compound, where there were at least forty Brown Locusts standing guard. She started from the far left and swept through the rank of assassins like a March wind. All forty collapsed awkwardly to the ground. The soundless night welcomed their silent deaths.

Moon Tao Po stood on the front lawn looking at the ninjas aligning the four balconies. She raised the sickles out to the sides, at shoulder level, and went into a cyclone spin, allowing her will to move her astral form. As one sickle severed their spirits from their souls, the other sickle annihilated the spirit altogether. Balcony after balcony, the Brown Locusts' lifeless corpses slumped over the railings and plummeted to the ground.

Shyan had worked her way around to each side of the house, leaving corpses behind her. Her last kill, she reached within her enemy's soul with her astral hand and snatched the spirit out of the body, before cutting it asunder. With that done, she returned to the front of the house on the doorsteps, where Sia and Moon were waiting.

Together, the three unseen assassins entered the house. They swept through room after room, purging. As they made it to the master bedroom, they heard intimate sounds coming from within.

The three angels of death seeped through the wall and walked out into the bedroom.

Sue Chou was grinding on top of her lover. Their exposed naked bodies stood out in the dim natural lighting within the room. As she reached her climax, Shyan, Sia, and Moon ripped through her soul with their ethereal blades. Her body collapsed on top of her young lover, who continued to thrust up inside of her lifeless corpse until he released inside.

The young man was too weak from the release to attempt to move, not that it mattered to the three death bringers. They slashed straight through Sue's body to claim his life as well.

"Masters Sia Po and Moon Tao Po, wait right here," Shyan said. "I shall return shortly." She walked straight through the side wall within the bedroom, over into the next room, where the general's sons sat playing video games. Without hesitation, she ended the four teenage boys' lives with a thrust of her ethereal short swords. Mission accomplished. Next, she returned to the master bedroom.

The silence throughout the Brown Locusts' compound defied the reason behind it. So much death would normally leave the mournful and outraged cries of spirits and souls without understanding, but not this time. It was the spirit and soul's essence that stained the three mercenaries of deaths ethereal blades.

***

General Chan and his escort had reached their destination. The driver parked near the high gates. The other car parked right behind them, and out of it came five Brown Locusts. Four more got out of the car with Chan.

As they approached the high gates, the gates opened and Yuri, along with two Green Mantises, stood on the other side, waiting to greet the general and his personal guard. Chan and his nine assassins bowed. Yuri bowed back, but the two who accompanied him remained motionless.

"Greetings, General Chan Chou," Yuri said, in the nicest voice possible. "Welcome to Sune's Estate. Right this way, please. Master Ma Sune is expecting you."

Chan and his escort walked through the open gates and followed behind Yuri and his escort. But not too close, since he didn't want to provoke a negative reaction from the Green Mantises. He came to a stop in front of Ma Sune's study.

"Right this way, General Chan," said Yuri.

The general started walking up the steps with his guards behind him. Before Yuri opened the door leading into the study, he turned around and noticed the Brown Locusts were planning on following Chan inside.

"General Chan Chou, no personal guards are allowed within Master Ma Sune's study," he told him. "They must remain outside."

Chan nodded, remembering the last time he'd come to her study. In Chinese, he told the nine ninjas to remain posted in front of the building while he went inside for the meeting. They bowed and stepped back down the steps, taking their stance next to the two Green Mantises.

"Go on, young master," Chan said, with a serious expression upon his face.

Yuri opened the door and gestured for Chan to enter. He entered, and Yuri closed the door behind them before continuing forward. They walked silently side-by-side down the short hallway. When they came upon the door of the study, Yuri stopped and knocked twice.

Ma Sune's voice could be heard from inside of the study "Enter," she beckoned in her native language.

Yuri opened the door and walked in before the general and bowed. "Master Ma Sune, General Chan Chou." He moved to the side and Chan entered the room.

"Thank you, Yuri." Ma Sune continued, "You may return to your training."

Yuri bowed. "As you wish, Maser Ma Sune." He turned around and left, and closed the door behind him. He walked out of the front door and bowed to the two Green Mantises. "Master Ma Sune requests that you return to your duties." He continued on down the steps and turned left.

The Brown Locusts were waiting on the two Green Mantises to walk off. Their attention was so focused on the two that they paid no mind to the environment, which was a fatal mistake. Like spiders climbing down a wall, the Green Mantises fell upon them. Five of them dropped dead immediately after being stabbed through the crown of their head.

Before the other four Brown Locusts could react, the two Green Mantises standing next to them drew their swords and cut them down. Quickly, they dragged the dead bodies out of sight. Another group came behind them sweeping the sand to cover the blood and signs of the struggle.

After all was done, Yuri came back around the corner. He walked back inside and knocked on the door of Ma Sune's study and entered. "Forgive me for disturbing you, Master Ma Sune and General Chan Chou," he said, while bowing, "but, Master Ma Sune, it is time for the evening ritual."

Ma Sune nodded. "Thank you, Yuri."

He bowed and walked out, but this time he left the door open.

Ma Sune looked at Chan. She knew he was anticipating her question. "General Chan Chou, this is the reason we've sat in silence the entire time. I don't discuss the kind of business we're here to discuss before partaking in something so sacred. Now, would you like to accompany me and be my guest at the evening ritual?"

Finally, the question he'd been waiting for. Chan nodded. "I will be honored to be your guest, Master Ma Sune."

"Then, let's be on our way," she said, while standing to her feet.

They exited the study and walked outside under the dimly lit skies. Chan quickly noticed his nine-man escort wasn't anywhere in sight. He frowned and turned towards Ma Sune. "Master Ma Sune, where are my men?"

She pointed towards a building. "General, they are enjoying the evening meal. Our custom is to have those who live in the shadows protecting our people enjoy their meal first, while we perform each daily ritual."

With a look of admiration on his face, the general nodded. "Now, that's what I call honor. When Green Mantis and Brown Locust unite, I look forward in adopting customs of the Sune Clan."

Ma Sune simply nodded in response to his statement. She led the way to the courtyard. As they walked, she proceeded to fill Chan in on what to expect, see, and feel during the ritual. She could tell by his body language that he was happy to be participating.

They made it to the courtyard's double doors. Ma Sune pushed them open and they entered. General Chan immediately noticed the four elders sitting on their mats in meditation. They looked up at him as he and Ma Sune walked by. He bowed to each one to show them the respect they deserved.

"He also noticed the three women sitting together on the platform, facing in the opposite direction. Ma Sune stopped walking when they reached the front row. She turned to Chan and said, "It seems like Yuri was a little off timing, General Chan Chou."

"No harm done, Master Ma Sune," he replied. He watched the three women who had stood to their feet. However, they continued to keep their backs toward them.

Ma Sune noticed him watching them. She pointed in their direction. "Do you see something you like, General Chan Chou?"

Not knowing how to take the question, Chan shook his head. "No, not in a dishonorable way, Master Ma Sune. However, I'm more curious as to what they're doing."

She nodded. "Well, why don't you ask them General Chan Chou."

At the third mentioning of his name, Saki, Nya, and Yishi turned a series of backwards flips until they reached Ma Sune and Chan and surrounded them.

Chan was amazed. "Is this part of the evening ritual, Master Ma Sune? If so, it's an interesting start."

The four elders: Mae, Ty, Nam, and Shang had stood to their feet. They walked over to where everyone else stood.

Ma Sune looked in Chan's eyes and said, "General Chan Chou, allow me to introduce you to my kindred spirits."

She left him standing in the center alone. The four elders extended their arms straight out in front of them. Saki, Yishi, and Nya reached inside the sleeves and pulled out the blades that were hidden up the sleeves of Mae, Ty, Nam, and Shang.

Ma Sune unsheathed her blades as she continued to talk. "My daughter, Master Yishi Sune, sister, Master Nya Sune, elders, Masters Shang and Mae Sune."

Chan started to feel uncomfortable and confused. There was still three she hadn't introduced. "Master Ma Sune, who are the other three."

She nodded in the direction of Saki. "This may come to you as a surprise, General Chan Chou. Meet my niece, Saki Po. Daughter of Khia Li Sune Po and Han Xi Po—two beloved masters of the blood oath sworn to by Po and Sune Clan."

Chan's eyes widened with fear. "Master Ma Sune, is this some kind of sick joke!"

Ma Za Sune let the other blade slide down her left sleeve and into her hand. Then she said, "Chan Chou, I'm Mae Za Sune. Master of Masters, Ma Sune, Nya Sune, and my belated daughter, Khia Li Sune Po. Your day of reckoning has come."

Chan's fear turned into rage. "Master Ma Sune, you cannot kill me! I'm a government official! Besides, my men—"

"Your men died while you were sitting with me in my study, General Chan. And, now, you shall join them in death."

With that being said, they began slashing away. They made sure Chan suffered a thousand cuts before dying.

Still in astral form Shyan, Sia, and Moon, stood by awaiting the moment when the spirit would descend or ascend. As soon as Chan's spirit departed from his mutilated corpse, Shyan, Sia and Moon thrust their ethereal blades through it, causing it to let out a deafening cry in the astral realm, before dispersing to nothingness.

***

Jennifer was awake. *Obviously, the surgery was a success because I'm still here,* she thought to herself, as she sat up on the side of the hospital bed. The bathroom was calling her name. Legs a little wobbly from being off of her feet for so long, she made her way to the toilet, dragging the IV along the way.

She sighed as the pressure left her kidneys. Done, she wiped herself, flushed the toilet, and washed her hands. Walking out of the bathroom, she looked up and saw Doctor Hadley sitting in the chair next to the hospital bed.

"Have a seat," he said.

Seemingly feeling a lot more comfortable on her feet than she'd felt just moments prior, she walked over to the bed and plopped down. "Am I going to live, Doctor Hadley?"

He laughed. "You have a clean bill of health, agent."

"That's music to my ears," she said, smiling.

"However," Doctor Hadley began to say, "I need you to take three of these a day for the next six months." He handed her six-blister pack of pills. "I want to be sure the cancerous cells didn't damage any of your white blood cells. Okay?"

"Roger that," she replied. " I'm ready for my flight now. I need to get back home and get my affairs in order."

The doctor tapped the railing of the bed. "Now that you're up and moving around, that can be arranged. As a matter of fact, I'll get on it immediately." He left the room in a hurry.

Jennifer picked up the television remote and turned it on. Thankfully, the embassy had international cable, because if not, she would've been lost. Remembering that she couldn't o read or speak Chinese reminded Jennifer of everything that had brought her to this point. *Tabitha Greene is the reason for all of this*, she thought to herself, *and Tabitha Greene and her allies will all pay.*

Not finding anything she cared to watch, she turned the television off and laid back on the bed. She started plotting her revenge. In her mind, anyone who had stood by Tabitha must also feel her pain. Even Angel, although she saved her life by letting her know she was sick with cancer.

They're all ruthless, heartless killers, Jennifer thought to herself. She was so shrouded within her desire for revenge, she didn't realize the doctor had returned. accompanied by Two military police men accompanied him holding her personal belongings.

"Jennifer," the doctor called her name to get her attention. "Your flight is being prepped. I had your personal things brought in just in case you wanted to shower before leaving."

"How long do I have to wait?" she asked the doctor.

He looked at his watch. "It's 1916 hours now. You have at least 45 minutes, agent."

Jennifer nodded. "Well, yes, I'd love to shower and freshen up."

"Well, let's take the extra luggage away," said Doctor Hadley. He took the IV needle out of her right arm and put a Band-Aid over the punctured wound.

The doctor and the two officers left the room, giving her the privacy she needed to get herself together. While in the shower, she reminisced about Tabitha and every intimate moment they had shared. The images were so raw in her mind, she could feel the heat rising between her thighs and the arousal within her pulsating sex. She tried to fight the sensational temptation of touching herself, but she couldn't.

She closed her eyes and allowed the scenes of their love making to replay itself like a movie. She rubbed up and down her clitoris the way she enjoyed it. She imagined it was Tabitha's hands touching her and not her own. She thrust two fingers inside of herself and stroked faster and faster until the release came. And with the release came tears and sobs.

"How could you, Tabitha?" Jennifer said aloud. What no one knew about Jennifer was, she had no self-control. She'd been admitted to a psychiatric ward after her last relationship, which ended up becoming a fatal attraction.

After she had come home and caught her ex-lover in the hot tub with someone else, she snapped. Jennifer had pulled her military issued firearm and emptied the whole clip in the other woman.

Afterwards, she grabbed her lover by the hair and dragged her into the kitchen, where she took a steak knife and stabbed her in the chest over one hundred times. She'd managed to clean up and dispose of all the evidence.

Jennifer got out of the shower with murder on her mind. She was set on Tabitha suffering the same fate as her ex-girlfriend. She dried off and got dressed. In sneakers, blue jeans, and a white tee-shirt, she walked out of the shower room ready to go.

She grabbed her belongings and walked out of the hospital room. Two military police were waiting and they escorted her to the helicopter. Before she boarded her flight, she looked up in the sky at the moon. It was a blood moon.

"Next time the moon is red, I shall have my revenge, Tabitha Greene. I swear," Jennifer said in a whisper. She boarded the helicopter and five minutes later, she was airborne.

***

Shyan, Sia, and Moon had returned to their physical bodies. They opened their eyelids just to close them again. They'd been outside of their physical form longer than either would have liked to have been, and it had drained their bodies of energy. Without giving it a second thought, the three master assassins allowed sleep to claim their bodies.

Everyone else had gathered in the courtyard as summoned by Ma Sune. They looked upon the dead corpse of Chan Chou with no emotion shown on their faces. Malice and Trent had taken the masks off and stood with everyone else. Mae Za Sune raised her sword stained by the blood of her enemy, above her head.

"Kindred spirits," Mae Za Sune began speaking, "this lifeless corpse before us belonged to the murderer of our people. We know Chan Chou lacked courage and we know he was a coward, therefore, it's evident that he did not act on his own free will when he murdered Masters Khia Li Sune Po and Han Xi Po. We know he was acting under the command of the High Council."

Mae Za Sune paused long enough to make eye contact with her daughter, Ma Sune. "Now, the greatest question must be asked and answered. Will not the High Council be devoured? Will not their blood be sacrifices offered to the spirit of the Black Dragon and Green Mantis?"

Taking in the words of her mother, Ma Sune nodded and replied. "The demise of the High Council is already being set in motion. Once they are no more, we shall establish a new council. And, elder and master of each clan shall sit at the council table."

Everyone present nodded in agreement with Ma Sune. With a mutual agreement in place and agreed upon, Chan's body was taken away to be disposed. They left the courtyard headed to their individual sleeping quarters.

Malice walked through the door of his room and immediately saw Shyan, Sia, and Moon sound asleep on the floor. Instead of turning on the light, he used the already lit candle to light three more, so he could move around without disturbing them.

Malice got his things together and took a shower. Afterwards, he lay on the bed deeply in thought. The war was almost over with, so tomorrow he would pitch the subject of a marriage ceremony to Mae Za Sune. Tired from the day's activities, he had fallen asleep much sooner than he'd anticipated.

Ma Sune had gotten out of the shower and sat down on the side of the bed. She really wasn't tired, so she decided to go to her study. When she entered, the first thing to catch her eye was the blinking light on the fax machine, letting her know she'd received an incoming fax. She pressed the receive button as she sat behind her desk and waited for the document to come through.

The machine hissed and buzzed as the document came through. As she began reading the note that came along with it, she suddenly got an idea. She called the number at the bottom of the page, and after the fourth ring, someone answered the phone.

"Hello? This is Zhia Mi Yang. How may I help you," said the feminine voice on the other end of the line.

Ma Sune leaned back in her chair. "Master Zhia Mi Yang, this is Ma Sune. I just retrieved your fax."

Zhia turned the volume of the television down. She didn't want to miss anything that would be said. "Yes, Master Ma Sune, I don't see any reason why we can't have a great business relationship. There has never been any bad blood between our clans."

While Zhia spoke, Ma Sune continued to look over the document. "This is true, Master Zhia Mi Yang. Listen, there are other matters I wish to discuss with you. What is your schedule looking like for tomorrow?"

Zhia paused for a moment, trying to recall if she anything of importance to handle the following day. "Nothing too important that I can't make arrangements to meet a new business associate. What time?"

"Tomorrow afternoon," Ma Sune replied, "and Master Zhia Mi Yang, I look forward to us being more than business associates after our meeting," she added before ending the call.

Zhia turned the television off and lay back on the bed in and allowed her mind to wonder. *What exactly does she mean by more than business associates*, she thought. She had never been with a man before in her life, and she did have a strange appetite for the same sex. The infinite possible meanings behind Ma Sune's statement made her more anxious than she already was. "Oh, well, I guess I'll find out tomorrow afternoon," she said, talking to herself out loud. Soon, she had drifted on to sleep.

CHAPTER TEN

Morning had come. Everyone stood in formation in the courtyard on the Sune compound. Nya was leading the morning ritual. Her movement was flawless.

Nya led them through the emotional state of an element and then prostrated. She did this for every element. The peace and calm within the energy about her spread throughout the courtyard and rested upon everyone. The feeling was glorious.

Finally, the ritual came to an end. After Nya prostrated for the last time, she remained on her knees. She raised her right hand, as a signal letting everyone know it was over and that it was time to go prepare for the morning meal.

Everyone stood to their feet and silently left the courtyard. Ma Sune, Saki, and Yishi stayed behind and went to Nya's side on the platform.

In silence, they sat on their knees watching the sun rise above the horizon. Although it was the Sune's custom not to speak until after the morning meal was over, there was an exception made for those who weren't partaking.

Ma Sune rested her hand on her sister's left shoulder. "Nya, is everything okay?"

Nya nodded. "Yes, Ma, all is well. I'll just be glad when this is all over. War is a game for fools who cherish the illusion of victory and never sees or understands the precious gifts that are forfeited."

Saki nodded and commented, "Aunt Nya, I totally agree with you."

Ma Sune and Yishi, also nodded in agreement. Ma Sune remembered what she had planned and spoke on it. "Let me run something by you all. Master Zhia Mi Yang, who is a member of the High Council was elected to a seat not long ago. She will be our guest this afternoon. Of course, she and I have legal business matters to tend to, but it's not the reason I've summoned her."

Yishi liked having the same view of things in the same perspective as her mother. So, she stated her thoughts on the matter.

"So, let me get this straight, mother. You're planning on using Master Zhia Mi Yang to gain access to the where abouts of the High Council's meeting place? Then what?"

Ma Sune cocked her head to the side, looking at her daughter admirably. "I wouldn't go so far as saying I plan to *use* Master Zhia Mi Yang. She will be the only survivor of the High Council if she cooperates. If she—" Before she could explain her point of view her phone rang. She pulled it out of her left pocket and answered without looking to see who the caller was. "Hello?"

"Good morning, Master Ma Sune. Have you tuned into the news this morning? There's a very interesting cover story," the male caller said.

Ma Sune sat the phone down on the platform and pushed the speaker button. "Head Master Hia Xan Tu, I wasn't expecting to hear from you so early. Anyway, no, I haven't watched the news in weeks. No need to when you're very informed."

Hia chuckled. "So true, Master Ma Sune, so very true." He paused momentarily to compose his thoughts. "Master Ma Sune, there are three seats open at the council table. It would be a great honor if you and two more of your choosing sat in those seats."

She looked around at the others and shook her head. "Head Master Hia Xan Tu, I shall give your request some thought. The next time I contact you, you shall have your answer."

Ma Sune ended the call, knowing the next time Hia heard from her would be during his death.

"Again, a game for fools," Nya commented. "Fear has blinded the man so much he's willing to give death an open invitation to come sit at his table.

Nya offered a silent prayer, prostrated, and stood to her feet. "I, personally, say we should've ended Jennifer's life while we had the chance. The illusion of love being betrayed in the mind of someone so unstable is dangerous. I think she's going to become a problem."

Yishi nodded in agreement. "Aunty Nya, I was thinking the same thing about the deceiver."

Ma Sune exhaled deeply. She knew what her sister and daughter were hinting at. "While in the process of destroying an immediate threat, we have unintentionally created another."

Saki nodded, understanding what was being said. "Well, let's cross one bridge at a time. If Jennifer decides to act foolishly, Master Moon Tao Po shall have to deal with her accordingly if, and when, that time comes. Now, let's go prepare for our guest, Master Zhia Mi Yang. We shall have her as a guest in a great performance that'll take the place of the afternoon ritual." Yishi, Nya, and Ma were each in favor of Saki's proposal.

"Cousin Saki, how about you and I be the performers? We can let our training be the source of everyone's entertainment," Yisha suggested as they were leaving the courtyard.

"As you wish, cousin," replied Saki.

Ma and Nya shook their heads in amusement as Saki and Yisha took off walking. "Ma, if those two girls' training don't scare Master Zhia Mi Yang into hiding, she'll surely accept whatever proposal you make," said Nya.

The two sisters scrolled through the compound having casual conversation until they reached their living quarters. They bowed to one another and went their separate ways to freshen up for the rest of the day's activities.

***

After the morning meal, Malice had pulled Mae Za Sune to the side and informed her about the marriage ceremony. For the first time in a long time she smiled, which was shocking to Malice. He didn't know how to respond.

She knew she had taken him by surprise. Yet, when she begun explaining the way the ceremony would be conducted, the smile faded back to her usual no-nonsense expression. After she finished giving him the rundown, Malice nodded and let her know he understood.

"So, Master Malice, have you decided a sun or moon you'd like for the event to take place," she asked?

"I'm thinking two suns after we've completed the tasks before us," he replied.

She bowed. "Very well then. It shall be set for two suns after the next."

He didn't bother asking Mae Za Sune how she'd come to the conclusion of when the war would be over. He simply nodded and thanked her before walking over to where Trent, Shyan, Sia, and Moon stood talking. Shyan took one good look at him, and knew something was up.

"Malice, what's going on," she asked?

He didn't hesitate in telling them about his and Shyan's marriage ceremony which was set to take place in three days. Trent gave him high-five and Moon patted him on the back. Shyan, on the other hand, pulled him into a passionate kiss. "I loved you too," she told him.

Trent had promised them he'd stay for the wedding, but afterwards he'd be on a flight back to Jersey.

Sia turned her gaze toward Moon to see if she'd mention having similar plans. When she didn't comment on what Trent had said, Sia then decided she'd come to her own conclusion. As Malice continued discussing the ceremony, Ma Sune entered the dining hall dressed in a flowing forest-green silk robe. She called out for everyone's attention, before speaking of the upcoming event.

She looked at her watch and saw that the time was 10:58 a.m. "Kindred Spirits, we shall have guests arriving in less than an hour. Master Zhia Mi Yang of the Yang Clan, whom we refer to as the Gold Tiger, shall be joining us this sun. We have decided that Masters Yishi and Saki shall entertain us all with one of their training sessions. So, prepare yourselves."

Mae Za Sune walked up to Ma and whispered in her ear. Ma Sune nodded and continued to speak. "Three suns from now, there shall be a wedding taking place between Masters Shyan Nun Sune and Malice. They shall be joined in matrimony according to our custom. Tomorrow, the remainder of our enemies shall perish. Until then, let us all enjoy the entertainment to come."

She looked back at the time. It was 11:38 a.m. She bowed and exited the dining hall. Walking in the direction of the high gates, she'd decided to welcome Zhia personally.

By the time she'd made to the gates, Zhia and her three personal guards were already on the grounds headed towards her. She was dressed in a golden silk body dress with six inch heels to match. Her guards were dressed in the gold and black tiger stripe ninja suits.

As the gates begin to open, Ma Sune bowed and welcomed them in.

Zhia's first impression was based on the fact that Ma Sune had come alone to greet her. It made her feel a lot more comfortable. She walked side by side with her, and the three guards followed behind them. Normally, a master would glance over their shoulder in such a situation, but not Ma Sune, and that only added to Zhia's intrigue all the more.

"Master Ma Sune, it's an honor to walk the grounds of the Sune Estate. So much history just waiting to be learned and understood," said Zhia.

Ma Sune continued to look straight ahead. "It's an honor having you as my guest, Master Zhia Mi Yang. We shall discuss our business later in my study. Right now, we have entertainment and then the noon meal. Hopefully, I'm not asking for too much of your time."

Zhia shook her head. "Not at all, Master Ma Sune. You're welcome to have all the time you request this sun."

Ma Sune stopped and turned to get a better look at her. After taking in her well-defined body and beauty, she resumed walking. "Great, Master Zhia Mi Yang. We shall make the best of this sun together."

"I'm looking forward to it," Zhia replied, as they brushed hands in a consensual way.

They came to the courtyard where everyone was already seated on the mats in the sand. Ma Sune told Khia she could direct the three Gold Tigers to the dining hall. There, they would partake in the noon meal with the Black Dragons and Green Mantises who weren't attending the performance. She instructed one of the Green

Mantises to escort them since they didn't know the way. With that taken care of, Ma Sune led her to the second row, where they sat side by side.

The elder, Ty Po, stood on the platform dressed in the royal jet-black silk garments of the Po Clan. He bowed before the audience. "Greetings, Kindred Spirits. First, I would like to welcome our guest, Master Zhia Mi Yang of the Yang Clan. I will not keep you waiting on the entertainment for this sun. I present to you Masters Yishi Sune and Saki Po, our entertainers this sun. Make no mistake. What you're about to witness is not an act. This is the true training of those who are of the Black Dragon and Green Mantis Spirits."

Ty Po stepped off of the platform and took his seat amongst the other elders on the front row. Zhia watched as Saki and Yishi walked in from opposite directions. Saki was dressed in a black ninja suit, and Yishi, in a forest-green ninja suit. Neither wore masks.

The two women bowed before the audience and then faced one another and bowed again. Without warning, the training began. Saki and Yishi stood toe to toe throwing punches, elbows, kicks, and knees. Their speed would cause one to become dizzy if they weren't careful. They blocked and countered one another's counters.

All of a sudden, the instruments of death came whistling through the air. Quickly, Saki and Yishi dove out of the way. They hit the ground several feet apart and continued rolling in the sand, evading the death as it flew toward them. Yishi rolled right and stood to her feet next to the weapon's rack.

She grabbed the twin swords from the rack and began batting away the ninja stars that were coming straight at her. Saki had rolled left to the weapon's rack on the opposite side. She chose the steel Bo staff and started sending the ninja stars to the sand around her. Both women were exceptional with the weapons they wielded.

Zhia was so entertained she could barely sit still. She stared at the scene before her without blinking.

Ma Sune took notice of her body language and she could tell that Zhia was amazed. She rested her left hand on Zhia's upper right thigh. “Are you enjoying yourself, Master Zhia Mi Yang,” she asked.

Zhia placed her right hand upon Ma Sune's left. She continued to watch Saki and Yishi fearlessly take on weapons of destruction as they maliciously thrown by unseen hands. “That I am, Master Ma Sune.”

Saki and Yishi continued to evade and counter the oncoming assault of razor sharp stars. They began walking towards each other. Looking directly in each other's eyes, they continued batting down the projectiles steadily being thrown at them. Once they reached one another, the stars ceased to rain down upon them. Zhia thought it was over, but quickly realized she was wrong when their weapons clashed, steel against steel.

Saki and Yishi went at it. They displayed the true fearlessness of a warrior, ruthlessness of a ninja, and skillfulness of a weapon master. They changed defensive and offensive roles several times before finally bowing to each other and their audience.

Sensing it was now over, Zhia stood to her feet, applauding the performance.

Ty Po walked back up to the platform and addressed the audience with a little humor. “Remind me, never to get on those two masters' bad side. Now, kindred spirits, let us go and enjoy the noon meal.” He bowed and walked off.

Ma Sune, with Zhia at her side, led the way to the dining hall. They talked about the performance, and Ma Sune told her it hadn’t been an act, but rather, the way her daughter and niece had always trained.

“You don't look old enough to have a daughter of that age,” Zhia complimented.

Outside of the dining hall Zhia saw the three Gold Tigers talking with two Black Dragons and Four Green Mantises. Their interaction made her feel more at ease. And when they Entering the dining hall and seeing the table already set put the icing on the cake. She felt right at home.

Yishi and Saki didn't partake in the noon meal, so Zhia was given the seat to Ma Sune's left. Everyone else was sitting in their usual seats.

The cooks and kitchen help served the food before taking a seat themselves. It was a wonderful lunch of stir fried brown rice, cabbage, onions, peppers and garlic baked bass and fried sweet potato pie.

After they were done eating, Ma Sune asked Zhia to join her in her study. They excused themselves and the two masters left the table. When they were inside the confinement of the study Zhia relaxed a little more.

"So, what are we here to discuss, Master Ma Sune?" she asked, as she sat on top of the desk facing Ma Sune.

"Our future," Ma Sune replied. "The High Council is about to fall. I seek to form a new one under no ruling family. Every clan shall have an elder and a master sitting at the council table to represent them."

Zhia nodded, already liking the idea. "What do you need from me? Surely you don't need any help bringing down the High Council."

Ma shook her head. "I have several needs for you to meet, Master Zhia Mi Yang." She looked her up and down, desiring what she saw before her. "I don't need your clan's help to bring down the High Council. I only need the location of their meetings. I can handle everything else from there."

Zhia pondered silently about what was being asked of her. She weighed the pros against the cons of her acceptance. She had to be sure that what accepting was more beneficial than not accepting. Confident that she was making the right decision, she took out her phone, deactivated the pass code lock, and handed it to Ma Sune.

"In my phone is all the information you need," Zhia said. "I'm curious to know about those other needs you have for me to meet, Master Ma Sune.

Ma Sune scanned through the contacts, location points, and numbers on the phone before tossing it over into the chair in front of her desk. "Are you willing to find out, Master Zhia Mi Yang?" she asked, as she walked up on her and rubbed on her thighs.

Zhia inhaled and exhaled. "Yes, Master Ma Sune, I'm willing and ready." She opened her legs wide, allowing Ma to stand in between them.

Ma Sune slid both hands beneath Zhia's dress and pulled her panties off. Zhia stood up and took off the body dress and bra, revealing her flawless golden-brown body. Next, Ma Sune relieved her body of the silks she was wearing as well. They kissed and rubbed one another's body affectionately.

Pausing briefly, they stopped just long enough for Ma Sune to clear the top of her desk off. Zhia laid down on top of it and Ma climbed on top of her. They kissed and moaned from the pleasant feeling of their bodies being pressed against one another's. Their sexes gently rubbed against each other as Ma Sune slid her body up and down on top of Zhia.

Zhia grabbed hold of Ma's soft firm buttocks and squeezed them gently, pressing their sexes closer together. Ma felt the heat of their passion rising to its peak. She slid up and down on top of Zhia faster and faster. Each woman moaned louder and louder in between kisses. Finally, their releases came and flowed simultaneously.

Ma Sune stood up and assisted Zhia as she rose to her feet. They continued to kiss and rub on each other's breasts until their heartbeats returned to normal and the sensational feeling that came with the release came to a calm.

"I hope this wasn't just a one-time thing, Master Ma Sune," Zhia said seriously, while getting dressed.

Ma Sune finished getting dressed and gazed at her intently. "Master Zhia Mi Yang, we have a future together. Unknowingly, you've just entered into a sworn blood oath. Your flesh has become my flesh. Your blood has become my blood."

Zhia kissed her passionately. "Well, let's get this business behind us so we can begin our future."

Ma Sune picked up Zhia's phone and sent a copy of the information she needed to her phone, before giving it back to her. Before leaving the study, they embraced and kissed once more.

Afterwards, she accompanied Zhia and the three Gold Tigers to the high gates. She and Zhia bowed to one another and said their goodbyes.

Quickly, Ma Sune returned to her study. She had one of the Green Mantises who stood outside to go get Shyan, Sia, and Moon. When they arrived, Ma Sune showed them the information she'd gotten from Zhia. She explained, in detail, the plan she had come up with.

By the time Ma Sune got to the part of her plan that dealt with calling the headmaster and taking him up on his offer, her phone rang. It was a private caller, so she knew it had to be him. "Head Master Hia Xan Tu, what brings you to call me at such an hour?" she answered the phone asking.

"The High Council is meeting tomorrow at sunrise," Hia replied. "Have you given consideration to my offer?"

Ma Sune paused to make it appear like she was contemplating. "Yes, Master Hia Xan Tu, I've reached my decision upon the matter. I, along with Masters Saki Po and Yishi Sune, accept your offer."

Hia gathered himself from the joyful feeling that had come over him then he spoke. "What a grand honor indeed, Master Ma Sune. I'm sending you the invite via GPS location now."

Ma Sune looked at the screen of the iPhone. The message icon popped up with one new message. She opened and read it. Then she compared it to the information she'd gotten from Zhia. It was identical in detail.

"Your invite just came through. We shall see you tomorrow at first sun, Head Master Hia Xan Tu," she said, with her thoughts elsewhere.

Hia hung up the phone. Ma Sune turned her attention back to Shyan, Sia, and Moon. "I think we should have a bite to eat and get some rest. We end this tomorrow at sunrise. Before the sun is fully over the horizon, the High Council will have ceased to exist."

All four women walked out of the study and over to the kitchen. They all carried a medium size platter of fruit out into the dining hall and sat at the table and ate. Afterwards, Shyan, Sia, and Moon went to her room. She let Malice know that Sia and Moon would be sleeping over.

Malice looked at the three women and held his hands out in front of him. "You three will get no argument out of me. I'll go chill with Trent for the night." He kissed Shyan on the lips. "And I'll see you when you get back, my wife to be." The, he left the room.

As Ma Sune was on her way looking for Saki and Yishi, she walked up on them watching Yuri train. Seeing him wield the three chain linked Bo Staff was a sight to see.

"Excuse me, Masters Yishi and Saki, but we have some very important business to discuss," Ma Sune interrupted.

Without saying a word, Saki and Yishi turned around and walked off with her. She explained to them the situation and what was going to take place at sunrise. They nodded, in agreement to accompany her and play the role. Besides, Saki had waited patiently for the day when she would see the man's face responsible for her parents' deaths.

After Ma Sune had gone over all the details with them, they retired to their rooms to get some rest.

***

Zhia was in the bathtub. For the first time in months, her body felt pleased and relaxed. The way they had made love was sensational. Never had she released at the same moment as a lover before.

Thinking about Ma Sune, she picked her phone up off of the side of the tub and sent her a text. Before she could sit the phone back down, it rang. Seeing who the caller was put a smile on Zhia's face.

"Hi lover," she greeted.

The passion in her voice caused Ma Sune to inhale and exhale deeply. "Why text when you can call me, my golden tigress?"

"Point taken," Zhia replied. "Is there anything I need to know other than what I've already been informed of by Head Master Hia Xan Tu?"

News travels fast, Ma Sune thought to herself before answering Zhia's question. “Yes, my love. Come alone. And be sure to sit between me and the masters who are coming with me physically. I'm telling you this because the Black Dragon and Green Mantis Spirit is coming with us. And they shall devour every living spirit’s inside who are not bound by blood.”

Zhia fell silent for a moment. “You mean there will be real shadow walkers there? I've heard of the esoteric arts of Ninja, but I've never met one who actually delved in it.”

Ma Sune sighed. “My love, you met three at my compound. Anyway, come alone and remember where to sit. All shall die by the weapons wielded by the shadow walkers except for us and the headmaster. Masters Saki, Yishi, and myself will personally bathe our blades in his blood. You can also wet your blade with his blood if you so desire my love.”

“Then, I shall, lover,” Zhia replied “Goodnight, Master Ma Sune.”

“Goodnight, Master Zhia Mi Yang,” she replied and hung up.

Zhia sat the phone back on the side of the tub. After another ten minutes had passed, she got out of the tub, dried off, and went to bed naked.

***

Jennifer had slept on and off during the helicopter ride back to the United States. After they landed and she gotten off with her luggage, she saluted the pilot, co-pilot and the marine who had ridden along just in case of a surprise aerial attack. They returned her salute and waited until she was safely inside the federal building before leaving. Although it wasn't her shift, she was still able to get clearance to the floor where she worked.

She got off the elevator on the fourth floor. She walked up to the receptionist desk and spoke to Sally, her daily relief. “Good evening, Sally,” Jennifer said politely. “How’ve you been?”

Sally Bridgewell was a thirty four-year-old, pleasantly built, five foot nine brunette. She worked the hours no one else wanted to work, but that's also why she got paid more and got more paid vacations.

She smiled at Jennifer. “I've been holding up fine, Jennifer. How was your trip to China? Did you enjoy yourself?”

Jennifer shook her head. “The trip was a disaster, Sally. The best part about it was the food, and the fact that I made it back home alive and in great health. But I need you to do me a favor.”

“Sure, Jenn,” Sally replied. “What you need?”

Jennifer scribbled a note on a sticky note and gave it to her. “Just in case I don't make it in on time in the morning, give this note to the director, and tell him I'll meet with him when I do come in.”

Sally took the note and stuffed it in her coat pocket. “I'll be sure to take care of this for you. Head on home and get some rest, Jennifer. And by the way, it’s good to have you back.”

“I'm glad to be back. I have a lot of work to do. Have a good one, Sally,” Jennifer said, and walked away. She got back on the elevator and rode down to the parking garage floor. There, she took out a set of keys and pressed the button on the key chain, causing the lights on a vehicle to flash on. It was her Lexus Coupe that Tabitha had no idea about.

Jennifer got in her car, after throwing her luggage in the back seat, and drove off. On the way home, she stopped by a gas station, fueled up, and bought a six pack of Natural Ice beer. And when she finally made it home, she sat on the couch in the den and downed beer after beer. She didn't stop sipping until she was on the last two cans.

The last time she’d drank a beer was after she killed her last lover and the other women. Now, here she was again, ready to kill another lover and all of her lover's friends. Why? Because she felt like they had turned Tabitha against her. Thinking about it, she tried calling Tabitha's phone, but to her surprise, all she got was the voice recording informing her that the number she had dialed had been changed, and was no longer in service, or disconnected.

“I'm going to kill you!” she yelled. She threw the phone against the wall and caused the screen to crack beyond repair.

Feeling the effects of the beer, she curled up on the couch and fell asleep.

CHAPTER ELEVEN

It was 4:30 a.m., and Ma Sune, Yishi, and Saki were on their way to the meeting with the High Council. Nobody was in the mood for talking due to the fact, they weren't used to talking early in the morning. But the silence between them was more than just a custom, it was a preparation silence of knowing what was before them.

They pulled up at the abandoned warehouse. Two ninjas in midnight-blue ninja suits opened the gates to let them pass through. Inside, on the grounds, Ma Sune, Saki, and Yishi immediately took notice of the high dollar vehicles. Most importantly, they noticed the personal guards of the different clan masters who were already inside. Ma Sune was relieved to see Zhia had listened to her, and not brought her personal escort.

The three women got out of the car. Ma Sune and Yishi wore forest-green women's pant suits, and Saki wore an all-black women’s business suit. All three carried their sheathed swords in the left hand. As they approached the entrance, they bowed in passing to the assassins standing ready to give their lives for their masters.

They entered the dimly lit room and stood behind the empty seats. Two were empty to the left of Zhia and one empty on her right. Ma Sune stood to her right, and Saki and Yishi stood to her left.

All of the other seats were already filled. For the first time in their lives, Saki and Yishi looked in the eyes of the headmaster of the High Council.

The headmaster stood to his feet, and the others followed his lead. “Masters Ma Sune, Yishi Sune, and Saki Po,” Hia began, “welcome to the High Council. I'm Head Master Hia Xan Tu. From my right to your left is Masters Yin Tzu, Vai Ki Hun, Chang Le, Chen Sao, Xul Yung, Hie Lang, Zhia Mi Yang, Bolo Shang, and Wen Chu. This council has always operated under the guidance of thirteen honored masters from different clans. Master Saki Po, your mother and father, Masters Khia Li Sune Po and Han Xi Po were amongst the most honored and greatest council members this council has had."

Hia sat back down at the head of the table. All except for Ma Sune, Saki, and Yishi sat down as well. "Masters Ma Sune, Yishi Sune, and Saki Po, the High Council members will cast their votes to elect you to a seat at the council table. It is law that neither of you are present at the casting of this vote, so I'm going to have to ask you to step out into the hallway."

The three women stepped out into the hallway. Ma Sune wondered where Shyan, Sia, and Moon were, but their whereabouts became crystal clear when the sound of bodies hitting the floor around them was heard.

Shyan, Sia, and Moon had already demolished the assassins who were outside. Now, the three shadow walkers were inside causing death to fall upon all they deemed unfit of life—that would be everybody within except those who were bound by blood oath. Every ninja lurking in the shadows fell to their deaths by the unseen instruments of death ripping, snatching, and severing their spirits from the body.

"It has begun," Ma Sune said in a whisper. "Prepare to put an end to our enemies last stronghold."

She unsheathed her sword. Saki and Yishi followed her lead. When they felt the presence of their kindred spirits enter the council room before them, they waited five minutes before rushing in. When they entered the council room, they immediately became aware of the eight dead council members with their heads on the table. Seemingly they appeared to be sleeping.

Hia and Zhia were the only two council members alive who sat at the table. The headmaster stood to his feet furiously. "What is going on here? I welcome you into my house and this is how you repay me!" He tried to make a run for it, but Zhia cut off his path by unsheathing her sword and putting the blade to his throat.

He looked at her with pure hatred in his eyes. "And you, Master Zhia Mi Yang! How dare you betray the High Council! I'll have you hanged for treason!"

"I don't think you'll be doing much of anything Hia Xan Tu," Ma Sune said, as she, Saki, and Yishi walked up on him with their swords poised, ready to cut him down. "Your day of reckoning has come. I promised the Spirits of the Black Dragon and Green Mantis that your blood would pour from your corpse before the sun rises fully above the horizon. And now my oath shall be fulfilled. Ladies?"

Saki and Yishi began slashing away at Hia's body. Zhia joined in the blood bath. With every slash from their blades, blood splashed in their faces and on their clothes. Hia cried out in pain, pleading for them to go ahead and kill him, but his plea fell upon deaf ears. They continued to hack at him, cutting him deep enough to cause blood to pour from the wounds, but not deep enough to kill him.

He fell to his knees, clothes soaked in his own blood. His body shook violently from the pain. Saki, Yishi, and Zhia had stopped their ruthless assault and sheathed their blades. They watched with malice written all over their faces, as he crawled right into Ma Sune's path.

Without hesitation, Ma Sune beheaded Hia. And as his body gave up the ghost, Shyan, Sia, and Moon devoured it, and went back to their physical bodies. Mission accomplished, Zhia, Ma, Saki, and Yishi walked out of the council room, blowing out the candles along the way. With every step, they passed death.

Back outside in the sunlight, they all took a deep breath and sighed. Still, as they looked around, there were corpses lying about as if death had come to them in a peaceful state. Ma Sune told Saki and Yishi to take her car, since she would be riding back with Zhia. They nodded and left.

After they pulled off, Ma Sune hopped in the front passenger seat next to Zhia. She kissed her hungrily. "My golden tigress, our future has begun."

Zhia put the car in gear. "I'm definitely looking forward to spending the rest of my suns and moons with you." She drove off, following behind Saki and Yishi.

***

Jennifer woke up with a chip on her shoulder. Her head was throbbing, and she was feeling depressed. Everything that reminded her of why she'd quit drinking in the first place. She took her medicine and made her way to the shower. She took a five minute cold shower to take the edge off.

Dressed and on her way out to work, she stopped by the master bedroom to grab her iPhone, but quickly remembered she'd thrown it and broke it against the wall. *Dumb shit. Another reason I quit drinking. Too emotional,* she thought to herself as she left the house.

She didn't bother turning the radio on in the car. She needed the quietness to prioritize her thoughts so everything would go as planned. She knew the first place she would have raided was the slaughterhouse. It was a key to her success.

Next, she pulled up to the security post, flashed her badge, and waited for clearance. The gates slid open and she drove through to the parking garage and parked in the western wing. She got out and walked over to the elevator with an air of confidence about her. She knew what she was set on doing and she planned to see it through.

She got off on the fourth floor. She walked out just in time to catch the director before he went in his office. "Director? Sir, may I please have a private word with you?"

He turned around to see Jennifer and smiled as she came walking up. "Well, good morning, Jenn. It's good to see you've made it back from Beijing in one piece. I got your note. Step into my office."

They stepped into his office and closed the door. The director took a seat behind his desk and gestured for her to have a seat in the leather chair before him. "Now, about this note of yours," he said, while pulling it out of his pocket. "Are you saying you would like for us to investigate this matter?"

Jennifer shook her head. "No, sir. I'm saying," she jotted down the location of the slaughterhouse on a memo on top of his desk, "go raid this place. I'm positive there was illegal activity going down inside. The people who own it are trained killers. Killers on a level you wouldn't believe."

The director chuckled. "Jenn, you don't have a clue of what I believe. Anyway, I'll send some guys over to check the place out. If your hunch pans out, we'll dig deeper to see what we can uncover. Cool?"

Jennifer nodded. "Of course, and thanks, sir." She walked out of the office, feeling victorious. She relieved Sally and thanked her for delivering the message.

The director peeped out of the door of his office. He looked at Jennifer with a look of disgust before closing and locking the door. He pulled out his personal phone and made an international phone call to China. The phone rang twice before the masculine voice came through the other end. "Hello?"

The director sat down and kicked his feet up on the desk. "Mr. Freeman, it seems we have a little problem."

"What kind of problem," asked Mr. Freeman.

"Jennifer came to my office a few minutes ago demanding that I send agents to raid the guild house," the director replied. "How do you propose I handle it?"

Mr. Freeman sighed out of frustration. "Director, do your job. Send the agents. Whatever they find is what they find. Don't jeopardize your position, brother. I have someone who will take care of the problem."

"Understood, Mr. Freeman," the director said. "Enjoy the rest of your vacation. Goodbye." He hung up. The director punched line one and gave the location to the slaughterhouse to the raid division and told them to go check it out. He sat back, relaxed in his chair and wondered just how far Jennifer was willing to go. One thing he did know was, she was digging her own grave. *Oh well,* he thought to himself.

The team of agents had made it to the slaughterhouse. The team leader called the director immediately after entering.

"Sir, this is Team Leader James Smith," he said once the director answered the call.

"What do you have for me, team leader," asked the director.

James looked around at all the decayed bodies along with the foul stench of death. "Sir, it looks like the pit of hell. Rotted corpses and more. It looks like a storm hit this place. Part of the ceiling is caved in."

The director sighed. "Alright, team leader. I'll get a team over there to clean up the mess. It's a federal investigation, so keep it hushed."

"Will do, sir," James replied and hung up.

The director stepped to the office door and asked Jennifer to step back in. Quickly, she jumped to her feet and hurried inside.

"Yes sir," she said enthusiastically.

"Looks like your lead checked out, Jenn." he said, trying to sound surprised. "We will launch a full scale investigation soon enough. You're dismissed."

Jennifer nodded, trying hard to keep her composure. She sat back down at her desk as happy as she could be. All she could think of was how fun it was going to be ruining Tabitha Greene's life.

***

Malice and Trent had talked about the situation concerning Jennifer. Neither was really upset because they knew the investigation would end in a ghost hunt, however, with Jennifer dead. They decided it wasn't even worth telling Shyan and Moon about. Not yet anyway.

"Besides, bro, I'm getting married in two days," said Malice. "Let's enjoy ourselves."

Trent nodded in agreement. "That's what's up, bro. When I find my queen, I'll be doing the same thing."

As they talked, Ma Sune, Saki, and Yishi scrolled into the dining hall. Their presence told Malice and Trent that the other three had returned also. It also told them that there wasn't a High Council any longer. The three masters took their seats at the dining table and waited to be served.

While they waited, Ma Sune stated the obvious. "The old High Council has fallen. The new High Council shall rise. We have avenged the blood of our fallen. Now we can live in peace."

The kitchen help brought them freshly brewed tea, straight out of the oven pancakes with warm raw honey syrup, and fried salmon patties.

Ma Sune, Saki, and Yishi ate their share before retiring to their rooms to rest.

Trent looked at Malice. “Well, I guess we can start getting you sized up for your death, I mean wedding.”

Malice covered his face so no one would see him chuckle. “You're a day late, bro. Mae Za Sune already handled that for me and Shyan.”

Trent shook his head in disbelief. “The woman stays a step ahead on everything.”

Malice nodded in agreement. “Trent, that's all women.”

He looked up and saw Shyan, Sia, and Moon entering the dining hall. “And speaking of women, here comes the bride and her ruthless sidekicks.”

Shyan, Sia, and Moon sat down at the dining table. It was easy to tell they were exhausted due to their demeanor. The kitchen help brought them food and drinks, which they made short work of. Without saying a word or making any real eye contact with anybody, the three women got up from the table and left.

Watching them exit the dining hall, Malice sighed with relief. “Man, I'm glad this is over. I'd rather deal with a hundred emotionally disturbed women like Jennifer than go through this again.”

Trent placed his left hand on Malice's right shoulder. “You said it. However, the vengeful heart is just that. A vengeful heart. Some hands just reach higher than others.”

The two men continued to carry on in casual conversation until Yuri walked up and bowed. “Master Malice and Trent, I would be honored if you sparred with me. I want to test my weapon proficiency.”

Malice and Trent were awed by the ten year old's articulate speech, but then they remembered they were in China. Malice bowed back to Yuri. “As you wish, Yuri.”

Yuri's eyes lit up. “Great. Let's go.”

They stepped outside and walked to the courtyard. Malice and Trent knew what Yuri's favorite weapon was, so they chose to grab Bo Staffs as well. Yuri stood in the sand barefoot with his three-chain link Bo Staff ready. Trent decided he would go first, but as soon as he stepped in front of Yuri, Yuri held out his left hand beckoning for Malice to come too.

"Master Malice and Trent, I'm ten in age, I'm not helpless. Let's begin," Yuri commanded, getting in his defensive stance.

Not wanting to dishonor Yuri, Malice and Trent, both, attacked. As Trent went for a backward leg sweep with the Bo Staff, Yuri leapt over the steel sweeping rod, and at the same time, blocked the downward slashing move made by Malice. He landed on his feet and continued to evade and block their attacks. They were beginning to have fun with helping Yuri train.

Yuri wielded the Bo Staff to the perfection. He whirled it around behind his back to block a strike coming from Malice, and leapt through the air, bringing the staff between his legs before sweeping upward to offset Trent's side thrust. They danced to the deadly tune of the steel clashing against steel for a good ten minutes. It didn't dawn on them that they had attracted an audience until it was over.

Yuri, Trent, and Malice bowed to each other before facing and bowing to their audience, who bowed back and nodded approvingly. Malice and Trent, both commended Yuri on his skillfulness and proclaimed they would be honored to fight alongside him. His eyes radiated but his nonchalant facial expression didn't. He bowed again and thanked them before walking off in high spirits.

The following day came surprisingly fast. After the morning ritual and meal, Ma Sune drove over to Zhia's office by the shipping dock. The two women sat in the office finalizing their business contract. She didn't even bother reading the contract because she trusted Zhia enough to just sign it.

Zhia stamped it and put her signature on it, and placed it in the active business files drawer. With the business complete, she told Ma Sune to follow her, she wanted to show her around and explain the way things worked. They walked side by side down the dock.

Every so often, she would stop and point at an operation and explain what was going on.

Like the Sune's Fabric Industries, Ma Sune quickly realized Zhia only employed members of the Yang Clan. Shipments were steadily coming in and going out. “This can be a crazy business sometimes,” Zhia explained. “Some gangs try to smuggle drugs in and out through shipments under their boss' companies. Then there are the sick bastards who are always getting caught trying to smuggle little boys and girls, selling them into prostitution.” She turned to look Ma Sune in the eyes and added, “And those individuals are the ones I deem unworthy of life. We catch them, torture them, and then kill them. Some people are undeserving of a quick and painless death.”

As Zhia was talking, one of the dock workers ran over to where she stood with a look of panic on his face. “Excuse me, Master Zhia, but I think you need to see this.”

She remained calm and introduced Ma Sune to the man. “Tham Dao Yang meet Master Ma Sune. Master Ma Sune, this is my cousin, Tham Dao Yang.”

She bowed. Tham bowed back and turned his attention back to Zhia. “I've just discovered another shipment of crates with children in them.”

Zhia's expression turned cold and her eyelids seemed to fall low. Her forehead suddenly displayed creases and on her face grew a frown. “Show us the crates.”

She and Ma followed Tham up the dock and onto a ship. Down in the fragile crates department, he opened the top of the crate, revealing ten young boys who looked like they were on the brink of starvation. Ma Sune couldn't hide her anger. “Who does this shipment belong to?”

Tham ripped the sticker off of one of the crates and read it. “It says here, property of the Tu Clan.”

“Thank you,” Ma Sune replied. “It's been a pleasant meeting, Master Zhia, but I must get going.”

Zhia, already knowing what Ma Sune had in mind, walked off the ship with her. “Wait. I'm coming with you.” She hurried in the office, grabbed her sword, and rushed back out behind Ma Sune.

They jumped in Ma Sune's Audi 8 and drove off. Zhia looked at her. “So, where are we going? Do I need to call and have some of the Gold Tigers meet us there?

Ma Sune shook her head, keeping her eyes on the road. “No, you don't need to call anyone. We're going straight to their main office near the mines, and I'm planning on slaughtering all office personnel.”

Zhia relaxed in the passenger seat. “I like your plan.”

Ma nodded and stomped the pedal to the floor. They made it to the main office of Tu's mining company in record time. Ma Sune parked right in front of the entrance and both women hopped out with their swords already drawn. They walked inside cutting the people down who just happened to be on their way out.

It was a real massacre. Ma Sune and Zhia walked through silently leaving bloody corpses in their path. They killed everyone, whether they were employees, employers, or customers. And amongst the dead was Mya Tu, the wife of Hia Xan Tu.

Ma Sune wiped the blood on her sword off on the dead woman's shirt before sheathing it. “Let's go.” she told Zhia.

The two made their exit just as quickly as they has made their entrance. Ma Sune sped back to the docks and dropped Zhia back off and told her if she needed any assistance with finding the kidnapped children a home to give her a call. The two women embraced and kissed before going their separate ways.

***

Mae Za Sune sat with the other elders, planning the wedding ceremony. They'd come to several conclusions: the layout, dress code and style. What they hadn't decided on was which one of them would preside over the ceremony. Since no one volunteered, Mae Za Sune accepted the responsibility.

I've already made most of the preparations, so why not do the honors as well, she thought. While they sat in the courtyard planning, she walked up on the scene and interrupted.

"Excuse me. I have just left the Tu's mining company's main office. All of their officials are dead." She was about to walk off, but another thought hit her. "And since there's a wedding tomorrow, cancel the afternoon and evening rituals."

All of the elders nodded. Ma Sune went on her way. She was still upset about the issue with the children. She shut herself up inside of her sleeping quarters after she'd made arrangements for her meals to be brought to her room—where she planned on staying until she got control of her emotions.

Ma Sune sat in the lotus position on her bed. She knew the best way to calm down was through meditation. During the meditation, she let her thoughts run wild. She gave up control only to gain it back with a greater sense of control.

After an hour and a half passed, a knock came at her door. Knowing it was kitchen help bringing her food she called out, "Enter!"

The help walked in carrying a tray with a portion of what was being served for the afternoon meal. After she thanked them, they nodded and left.

While Ma Sune ate, she thought about the best possible way to approach the other clans with her idea. She knew it was a wonderful plan but she also knew some of the clans were into illegal activities like the Tu Clan was. As she thought about it even more, she realized she needed the help of someone who knew and dealt with all clans. So, she picked up her phone and called Zhia.

Zhia answered the call on the first ring. "Hello?"

"Master Zhia Mi Yang, this is Master Ma Sune," she said. "I need your professional advice on a matter."

"I'm listening," Zhia replied, giving her undivided attention.

"What clans are not into illegal businesses?" asked Ma Sune.

Zhia paused for moment, looking through the file drawers, until she found the documents she was searching for. She held the document that listed all clan names as well as their formal, informal and seized business contracts due to illegal activity. She read the list of all the notable, honorable clans to Ma Sune. "As you can see, Master Ma Sune, there are fewer honorary clans than there are dishonorable ones."

It was kind of what Ma Sune was anticipating. "Okay, Master Zhia Mi Yang. Now, I have one more task for you to complete as soon as possible. Send an invite to all of the honorary clans to attend the wedding tomorrow."

"No problem," Zhia stated, while turning to her computer. "What time does everyone need to be there?"

Ma Sune thought for a moment. "The ceremony will officially begin at 11:45 a.m., therefore, the guests need to arrive around 11 a.m."

Zhia typed in the invite and linked it to the email of each clan's master. She clicked send and said, "Done. What time do I need to arrive?" she wanted to know.

Ma sighed. "Be here before everyone else. How about that?" she said, before hanging up.

Her plan was coming together. "Soon all clans true to the way would be united," she said to herself.

After talking to Khia, Ma Sune's appetite for food was no longer present. Now, she hungered for her along with the craving to seeing her plan through successfully.

***

Jennifer was officially off the clock, on the other hand, she was unofficially doing her own research. She sat at home on her computer doing a background research on Tabitha's family. So far, all she'd found was dead-end stories. The status quo of a typical family.

Remembering Tabitha's belongings were still there, she began rambling through her personal paperwork. While looking, she stumbled upon her birth certificate and social security card. She closed out of the files she was in and typed in Tabitha's social security number and date of birth. When she pressed enter, nothing happened.

Not having the luck, she was hoping for, she could feel herself getting frustrated. She exited out of all running apps on the computer and typed in her federal clearance passcode. After access was granted, she pulled up the search engine again and typed in Tabitha's information again. This time, the warning icon popped up and covered the entire screen.

Jennifer tapped the enter button twice. Finally, a file document popped up, but it wasn't to her liking. According to the document on the screen, nobody even existed with the said social security number and date of birth. “So, everything you've told me was a lie, Tabby,” she said to herself, becoming angrier by the minute.

She was about to log off when the computer went through a rebooting of its own. After the home screen popped back up, she checked to make sure she'd logged out of the federal data bank. But when she tried to pull up the file using her passcode, her access was denied. Jennifer frowned and tried again and again and continued to get the same response of access denied.

Now she was furious. Someone had revoked her clearance. She shut down the computer and unplugged it. Somehow, she felt like Tabitha had saw her snooping around in her personal things and blocked all of her personal information from being viewed by the public.

But that doesn't make any sense, she thought. She laughed deliciously. It didn't really matter because she knew all the details she needed to know to bring Tabitha down for good.

CHAPTER TWELVE

The big moment was fast approaching for Malice. It was 11:15 a.m. In thirty minutes, he would be taking the biggest step in his life. At least, that's how he was thinking anyway.

He and Trent stood near the entrance of the courtyard talking. Trent could tell he was nervous and anxious to get it done and over with. He gave Malice the best pep talk he could, being that he, himself, had never been married. Trent couldn't even recall ever being in love, and the one woman he could've possibly fallen in love with was Valencia.

He looked at his watch. The time was 11: 30 a.m. "Alright, Champ, let's do this. The ceremony starts in fifteen minutes. We need to already be standing on the platform by then."

Nervousness mixed with anxiousness consumed him, and Malice rubbed the palms of his hands together. "You're right, bro. Let's do this."

They walked down the aisle, bowing to everyone as they passed by. Every clan Zhia sent the invite to, their masters had shown dressed in their elaborate robes and gowns. The audience was a colorful sight. It was exactly what Ma Sune had hoped for.

By the time Malice and Trent reached the platform, Shyan stood dressed in the most beautiful forest-green silk gown money could buy. Moon, Mae Za Sune, Ty Po, Nam Wang Po, and Shang Sune were all in attendance and it was time for the ceremony to begin.

Mae Za Sune stood out front and addressed the audience. "Kindred Spirits, it is a blessing to see you on this sun helping us celebrate the birth of a new life. This sun we shall partake in the unification of spirit, soul, mind, and body. We shall all be witnesses of a new sworn blood oath."

She bowed respectfully and turned to face Shyan and Malice. The two stood facing one another, staring into one another's eyes deeply. "Master Shyan Nun Sune and Malice, our tradition does not cause for the oath of word, but the oath of blood alone. Are you willing and ready, to take and swear to this blood oath?"

Both nodded silently. Mae Za Sune gestured for Ty Po, and Shang Sune, the elders who carried gold platters with golden chalices and ceremonial daggers on them, to come forth.

Ty Po asked Malice to hold out his left hand. And, when he did, Ty Po sliced through his palm deep enough to cause blood to flow. He held the golden chalice beneath Malice's bleeding hand to catch the blood. Once the bleeding slowed to a droplet, he sat the chalice on the platter next to the ceremonial dagger and sat the platter down on the platform. Next, he tied a black silk scarf around the wound. He picked the platter back up and handed Mae Za Sune the golden chalice.

At the same time, Shang Sune had gone through the same process with Shyan.

Mae Za Sune raised the two chalices above her head. "Now we call upon our ancestral spirits to witness, partake in, and be in agreement with this blood oath that shall bind us all." She gave Shyan the golden chalice with Malice's blood in it and in turn handed him hers. "If it truly be thine will, drink and fulfill your oneness."

Shyan and Malice didn't hesitate. They turned the cups of blood up and didn't turn it down until the cups were empty of the essense. Ty and Shang retrieved the golden chalices and nodded to bear witness to their fulfillment. Mae Za Sune nodded approvingly.

"As it is known, what is bound by blood cannot be undone. Masters Shyan Nun Sune and Malice are now one in spirit, soul, mind, and body. The blood oath given allows them to truly know one another's emotions and thoughts. They have been reborn within one another this sun. We who are here witnessing and agreeing are reborn within them as well. We are all now under the blood oath."

Mae Za Sune bowed before walking over to stand with Ty, Shang, and Nam. They began to privately confer about another matter.

Malice closed the gap between him and his wife, Shyan. "The moment I've been waiting for," he said as he took her in his arms and kissed her.

Mae just so happened to look up. Seeing them kissing, she hurried up with their little conference, walked over, and tapped Malice on the shoulder. "Excuse me, Master Malice, but that time has not come yet."

He had to force himself to pull away from Shyan's soft lips. For the second time, he saw Mae smile. She grabbed his left hand and Shyan's right and faced the audience.

"Kindred Spirits," Mae Za Sune said, "the spirit of the Green Mantis has spoken. Master Malice will no longer be known as Malice. As he has been reborn through matrimony, so has he in name. From now on, from this sun forth, he is Master Sun Sa Sune." She turned to him and asked, "Do you accept and embrace the will of the spirit of the Green Mantis, my son?"

He bowed and replied, "Yes, and I'm honored to."

"Then proclaim your name, my son," she said.

"From this sun forth," Malice began saying, "my name is no longer Malice or Kenneth Freeman. I am Master Sune Sa Sune!"

"Now, you may kiss the bride," Mae said, as she let go of their hands and walked off the platform.

"Round two," Shyan said, before leaning into his kisses.

The clans cheered them on. With the wedding ceremony over, Ma Sune walked on to the platform. She hugged Shyan and bowed to Sun before addressing the clans. "Kindred Spirits of honorable clans, the glory of this sun must continue. If you are still unaware of the fall of the High Council, I am making you aware of it now. The headmaster Hia Xan Tu and his underlings are dead."

There was a look of surprise, mixed with relief, on everyone's face who didn't know. Ma Sune noticed it and continued to deliver her proposal. "Now, we the honorable clans born of China, shall form our own council. Two masters and two elders from each clan shall represent the voice of their clan. We shall develop our own social, economic, and government according to our customs. Most importantly, we shall remain discipline in the way of Ninja."

She signaled for the Green Mantises to come forth carrying the written documentation of a new High Council under the rule of the clans. "All that is required is your signature in blood."

Without delay, Ma Sune pricked her thumb on the point of her dagger and pressed it against the document. Saki followed her lead, and Zhia after her. All of a sudden, the other masters from the different clans silently followed suit and gave their sworn signatures as well.

"It has begun," Ma Sune proclaimed, while gesturing for the Green Mantises to return the documents to her study. "We are all sworn under the blood oath to live as one. The wedding dinner is ready. Let us go eat together, as the united family we are."

They began leaving the courtyard, heading for the dining hall, where they had placed two more tables the same length as the one already there. Everyone sat down and enjoyed their meal. After the feast and all of the guests had left, Trent pulled Sun Sa Sune to the side and told him he was about to leave. The two mercenaries embraced each other with brotherly love.

"Take care of yourself, bro, and don't hesitate to hit me up if you need me," Sun said.

"Bro, I'll see you back in the states when you and the wifey return," Trent replied, and headed for his room. He packed up and left without saying goodbye. By the time Shyan and Moon knew he was gone, he was already in the cab, heading to the airport to catch his flight.

***

Jennifer had rebooted her computer again after work. She had complained to the director about her access being revoked. She also made him aware of the fact that she believed Tabitha Greene and her mercenary friends were responsible. The director had gotten exhausted to the point that he reinstated her access without her knowing. Afterwards, he had given her an early leave to see if her pass code worked on her computer at home.

So, here she was waiting on the home screen to pop up. And when it did, she typed in her federal pass code and it worked. The first thing she became aware of was the new message in the notification box. She clicked on the icon to read it.

When the notification box opened on the screen, Jennifer smiled. “I got you, buddy,” she said maliciously. The notification was of Trent's flight back to Jersey.

Jennifer had used her contacts at the airline’s headquarters to set up an account letting her know when certain people were boarding flights and what their destination was. Trent just so happened to be one of those people.

To Be Continued. . .
Ruthless Hearts 3
Coming Soon

Submission Guideline

Submit the first three chapters of your completed manuscript to ldpsubmissions@gmail.com, subject line: Your book's title. The manuscript must be in a .doc file and sent as an attachment. Document should be in Times New Roman, double spaced and in size 12 font. Also, provide your synopsis and full contact information. If sending multiple submissions, they must each be in a separate email.

Have a story but no way to send it electronically? You can still submit to LDP/Ca$h Presents. Send in the first three chapters, written or typed, of your completed manuscript to:

LDP: Submissions Dept
Po Box 870494
Mesquite, Tx 75187

DO NOT send original manuscript. Must be a duplicate.

Provide your synopsis and a cover letter containing your full contact information.

Thanks for considering LDP and Ca$h Presents.

Coming Soon from Lock Down Publications/Ca$h Presents

BOW DOWN TO MY GANGSTA

By **Ca$h**

TORN BETWEEN TWO

By **Coffee**

THE STREETS STAINED MY SOUL **II**

By **Marcellus Allen**

BLOOD OF A BOSS **VI**

SHADOWS OF THE GAME II

By **Askari**

LOYAL TO THE GAME **IV**

By **T.J. & Jelissa**

A DOPEBOY'S PRAYER **II**

By **Eddie "Wolf" Lee**

IF LOVING YOU IS WRONG… **III**

By **Jelissa**

TRUE SAVAGE **VII**

MIDNIGHT CARTEL II

DOPE BOY MAGIC III

By **Chris Green**

BLAST FOR ME **III**

DUFFLE BAG CARTEL **IV**

A SAVAGE DOPEBOY III

By **Ghost**

A HUSTLER'S DECEIT III

KILL ZONE **II**

BAE BELONGS TO ME III

SOUL OF A MONSTER III

By **Aryanna**

THE COST OF LOYALTY **III**

By **Kweli**

CHAINED TO THE STREETS II

By **J-Blunt**

KING OF NEW YORK V

COKE KINGS IV

BORN HEARTLESS IV

By **T.J. Edwards**

GORILLAZ IN THE BAY V

De'Kari

THE STREETS ARE CALLING II

Duquie Wilson

KINGPIN KILLAZ IV

STREET KINGS III

PAID IN BLOOD III

CARTEL KILLAZ IV

Hood Rich

SINS OF A HUSTLA II

ASAD

TRIGGADALE III

Elijah R. Freeman

KINGZ OF THE GAME V

Playa Ray

SLAUGHTER GANG IV

RUTHLESS HEART III

By Willie Slaughter

THE HEART OF A SAVAGE II

By Jibril Williams

FUK SHYT II

By Blakk Diamond

THE DOPEMAN'S BODYGAURD II

By Tranay Adams

TRAP GOD II

By Troublesome

YAYO III

A SHOOTER'S AMBITION II

By S. Allen

GHOST MOB

Stilloan Robinson

KINGPIN DREAMS II

By Paper Boi Rari

CREAM

By Yolanda Moore

SON OF A DOPE FIEND II

By Renta

FOREVER GANGSTA II

By Adrian Dulan

LOYALTY AIN'T PROMISED

By Keith Williams

THE PRICE YOU PAY FOR LOVE II

By Destiny Skai

THE LIFE OF A HOOD STAR

By Rashia Wilson

TOE TAGZ II

By Ah'Million

CONFESSIONS OF A GANGSTA II

By Nicholas Lock

PAID IN KARMA II

By **Meesha**

I'M NOTHING WITHOUT HIS LOVE II

By Monet Dragun

CAUGHT UP IN THE LIFE II

By Robert Baptiste

NEW TO THE GAME II

By **Malik D. Rice**

Available Now

RESTRAINING ORDER **I & II**

By **CA$H & Coffee**

LOVE KNOWS NO BOUNDARIES **I II & III**

By **Coffee**

RAISED AS A GOON I, II, III & IV

BRED BY THE SLUMS I, II, III

BLAST FOR ME I & II

ROTTEN TO THE CORE I II III

A BRONX TALE I, II, III

DUFFEL BAG CARTEL I II III

HEARTLESS GOON I II III IV

A SAVAGE DOPEBOY I II

HEARTLESS GOON I II III

DRUG LORDS I II III

By **Ghost**

LAY IT DOWN **I & II**

LAST OF A DYING BREED

BLOOD STAINS OF A SHOTTA I & II III

By **Jamaica**

LOYAL TO THE GAME

LOYAL TO THE GAME II

LOYAL TO THE GAME III

LIFE OF SIN I, II III

By **TJ & Jelissa**

BLOODY COMMAS I & II

SKI MASK CARTEL I II & III

KING OF NEW YORK I II,III IV

RISE TO POWER I II III

COKE KINGS I II III

BORN HEARTLESS I II III

By **T.J. Edwards**

IF LOVING HIM IS WRONG…I & II

LOVE ME EVEN WHEN IT HURTS I II III

By **Jelissa**

WHEN THE STREETS CLAP BACK I & II III

By **Jibril Williams**

A DISTINGUISHED THUG STOLE MY HEART I II & III

LOVE SHOULDN'T HURT I II III IV

RENEGADE BOYS I II III IV

PAID IN KARMA

By **Meesha**

A GANGSTER'S CODE I &, II III

A GANGSTER'S SYN I II III

THE SAVAGE LIFE I II III

CHAINED TO THE STREETS

By J-Blunt

PUSH IT TO THE LIMIT

By **Bre' Hayes**

BLOOD OF A BOSS **I, II, III, IV, V**

SHADOWS OF THE GAME

By **Askari**

THE STREETS BLEED MURDER **I, II & III**

THE HEART OF A GANGSTA I II& III

By **Jerry Jackson**

CUM FOR ME

CUM FOR ME 2

CUM FOR ME 3

CUM FOR ME 4

CUM FOR ME 5

An **LDP Erotica Collaboration**

BRIDE OF A HUSTLA **I II & II**

THE FETTI GIRLS **I, II& III**

CORRUPTED BY A GANGSTA I, II III, IV

BLINDED BY HIS LOVE

THE PRICE YOU PAY FOR LOVE

By **Destiny Skai**

WHEN A GOOD GIRL GOES BAD

By **Adrienne**

THE COST OF LOYALTY I II

By Kweli

A GANGSTER'S REVENGE **I II III & IV**

THE BOSS MAN'S DAUGHTERS

THE BOSS MAN'S DAUGHTERS II

THE BOSSMAN'S DAUGHTERS III

THE BOSSMAN'S DAUGHTERS IV

THE BOSS MAN'S DAUGHTERS **V**

A SAVAGE LOVE **I & II**

BAE BELONGS TO ME I II

A HUSTLER'S DECEIT I, II, III

WHAT BAD BITCHES DO I, II, III

SOUL OF A MONSTER I II

KILL ZONE

By **Aryanna**

A KINGPIN'S AMBITON

A KINGPIN'S AMBITION **II**

I MURDER FOR THE DOUGH

By **Ambitious**

TRUE SAVAGE

TRUE SAVAGE II

TRUE SAVAGE **III**

TRUE SAVAGE **IV**

TRUE SAVAGE **V**

TRUE SAVAGE **VI**

DOPE BOY MAGIC I, II

MIDNIGHT CARTEL

By **Chris Green**

A DOPEBOY'S PRAYER

By **Eddie "Wolf" Lee**

THE KING CARTEL **I, II & III**

By **Frank Gresham**

THESE NIGGAS AIN'T LOYAL **I, II & III**

By **Nikki Tee**

GANGSTA SHYT **I II &III**

By **CATO**

THE ULTIMATE BETRAYAL

By **Phoenix**

BOSS'N UP **I , II & III**

By **Royal Nicole**

I LOVE YOU TO DEATH

By Destiny J

I RIDE FOR MY HITTA

I STILL RIDE FOR MY HITTA

By **Misty Holt**

LOVE & CHASIN' PAPER

By **Qay Crockett**

TO DIE IN VAIN

SINS OF A HUSTLA

By **ASAD**

BROOKLYN HUSTLAZ

By **Boogsy Morina**

BROOKLYN ON LOCK I & II

By **Sonovia**

GANGSTA CITY

By **Teddy Duke**

A DRUG KING AND HIS DIAMOND I & II III

A DOPEMAN'S RICHES

HER MAN, MINE'S TOO I, II

CASH MONEY HO'S

By Nicole Goosby

TRAPHOUSE KING **I II & III**

KINGPIN KILLAZ I II III

STREET KINGS I II

PAID IN BLOOD **I II**

CARTEL KILLAZ I II III

By **Hood Rich**

LIPSTICK KILLAH **I, II, III**

CRIME OF PASSION I II & III

By **Mimi**

STEADY MOBBN' **I, II, III**

THE STREETS STAINED MY SOUL

By **Marcellus Allen**

WHO SHOT YA **I, II, III**

SON OF A DOPE FIEND

Renta

GORILLAZ IN THE BAY **I II III IV**

DE'KARI

TRIGGADALE I II

Elijah R. Freeman

GOD BLESS THE TRAPPERS I, II, III

THESE SCANDALOUS STREETS I, II, III

FEAR MY GANGSTA I, II, III

THESE STREETS DON'T LOVE NOBODY I, II

BURY ME A G I, II, III, IV, V

A GANGSTA'S EMPIRE I, II, III, IV

THE DOPEMAN'S BODYGAURD

Tranay Adams

THE STREETS ARE CALLING

Duquie Wilson

MARRIED TO A BOSS… I II III

By Destiny Skai & Chris Green

KINGZ OF THE GAME I II III IV

Playa Ray

SLAUGHTER GANG I II III

RUTHLESS HEART I II

By Willie Slaughter

THE HEART OF A SAVAGE

By Jibril Williams

FUK SHYT

By Blakk Diamond

DON'T F#CK WITH MY HEART I II

By Linnea

ADDICTED TO THE DRAMA I II III

By Jamila

YAYO I II

A SHOOTER'S AMBITION

By S. Allen

TRAP GOD

By Troublesome

FOREVER GANGSTA

By Adrian Dulan

TOE TAGZ

By Ah'Million

KINGPIN DREAMS

By Paper Boi Rari

CONFESSIONS OF A GANGSTA

By Nicholas Lock

I'M NOTHING WITHOUT HIS LOVE

By Monet Dragun

CAUGHT UP IN THE LIFE

By Robert Baptiste

NEW TO THE GAME

By **Malik D. Rice**

BOOKS BY LDP'S CEO, CA$H

TRUST IN NO MAN
TRUST IN NO MAN 2
TRUST IN NO MAN 3
BONDED BY BLOOD
SHORTY GOT A THUG
THUGS CRY
THUGS CRY 2
THUGS CRY 3
TRUST NO BITCH
TRUST NO BITCH 2
TRUST NO BITCH 3
TIL MY CASKET DROPS
RESTRAINING ORDER
RESTRAINING ORDER 2
IN LOVE WITH A CONVICT

Coming Soon

BONDED BY BLOOD 2
BOW DOWN TO MY GANGSTA

CPSIA information can be obtained
at www.ICGtesting.com
Printed in the USA
LVHW022153170720
661013LV00010B/643